DEATH IN THE NIGHT!

Longarm drew his side arm and advanced on the confusion, getting there just as two dark blurs were backing out of his stateroom through a cloud of gunsmoke. So he demanded they freeze and fired almost in the same moment. He hit the nearest one and suspected he knew who it was as his target dropped faster than its big hat. He put another round in the son of a bitch before pegging his fifth and last shot at the sound of the other one's thudding boot heels . . .

SPECIAL PREVIEW!

Turn to the back of this book for a special excerpt from the riveting new Western by Gene Shelton . . .

Texas Horsetrading Co.

. . . A rousing epic novel of the Wild West from the acclaimed author of *Texas Legends*.

Available now from Diamond Books!

D1466989

DON'T MISS THESE
ALL-ACTION WESTERN SERIES
FROM THE BERKLEY PUBLISHING GROUP

THE GUNSMITH by J. R. Roberts
> Clint Adams was a legend among lawmen, outlaws, and ladies. They called him . . . the Gunsmith.

LONGARM by Tabor Evans
> The popular long-running series about U.S. Deputy Marshal Long—his life, his loves, his fight for justice.

LONE STAR by Wesley Ellis
> The blazing adventures of Jessica Starbuck and the martial arts master, Ki. Over eight million copies in print.

SLOCUM by Jake Logan
> Today's longest-running action Western. John Slocum rides a deadly trail of hot blood and cold steel.

◆→ TABOR EVANS ◆→

LONGARM

ON THE FEVER COAST

JOVE BOOKS, NEW YORK

LONGARM ON THE FEVER COAST

A Jove Book / published by arrangement with
the author

PRINTING HISTORY
Jove edition / March 1994

All rights reserved.
Copyright © 1994 by Jove Publications, Inc.
Texas Horsetrading Co. excerpt copyright © 1994 by
Charter Communications, Inc.
This book may not be reproduced in whole
or in part, by mimeograph or any other means,
without permission. For information address:
The Berkley Publishing Group,
200 Madison Avenue,
New York, New York 10016.

ISBN: 0-515-11338-7

A JOVE BOOK®
Jove Books are published by The Berkley Publishing Group,
200 Madison Avenue, New York, New York 10016.
JOVE and the "J" design are trademarks
belonging to Jove Publications, Inc.

PRINTED IN THE UNITED STATES OF AMERICA

10 9 8 7 6 5 4 3 2 1

LONGARM

ON THE
FEVER COAST

Chapter 1

The funeral seemed at least as dignified and twice as sober as anyone was likely to remember the late Justice Elroy Bryce of the Denver Probate Court. His Honor had been one of those sneaky old drunks who'd never taken a false step, slurred one word, nor made a whole lot of sense as he'd presided over mostly routine cases.

Longarm had appeared before His Honor a time or two to ask if they could use a dead outlaw's own pocket money to bury him decently, the outlaw being intestate, and old Elroy had been neighborly enough. But U.S. Deputy Marshal Custis Long, as he was known officially, was there at the funeral more as a representative of his federal court. Nobody but his immediate superior, U.S. Marshal William Vail, would come right out and say what they thought of the poor old political hack. But Longarm felt sure he'd been stuck with the chore because he was well known to the locals gathered in the church as a federal man, thanks to those dumb features about him in the *Rocky Mountain News* and *Denver Post*. Things had gotten to where a lawman wound up on the infernal front pages every time he had to gun a foolish road agent. It felt dumb to be sitting up front, in a fresh-pressed tweed suit and cruelly starched white shirt, for Pete's sake, while some jasper a row back whispered, "That's the one they call Longarm, and I'll bet that's his famous .44–40 bulging under the left tail of his frock coat."

Longarm wondered what else they expected a lawman on duty to be wearing cross-draw in such an uncertain world, especially after putting many an owlhoot rider in jail, or in the ground, while packing a badge for six or eight years. Judges made enemies along the way as well. In addition, a pesky reporter had gotten a look at the guest invitations, and printed in his paper how the notorious Custis Long would show up.

Longarm had managed to crawfish out of being a pallbearer, with hardly a chance in the world if some sore loser threw down on him while he was helping to carry the coffin. But he still itched far more between his shoulder blades than that pesky starch called for. It was taking the preacher a million years to take his place at that damned pulpit and get cracking. Meanwhile, all sorts of suspicious characters filed by, supposedly to pay their last respects to that old dead drunk in that open mahogany casket.

The church organ wasn't doing a thing to speed things up. Longarm couldn't tell whether the short and pleasantly plump brunette over in the alcove was playing hunt-and-peck on the organ keys because she couldn't make out the score propped up so high, or because she couldn't reach the pumping pedals slung so low with her little legs. She was seated at such a sideways angle that he couldn't quite make out just what she was really up to. Nevertheless, she or anybody else seated at her organ had a clear shot at most anyone filing past that old dead drunk. So Longarm rose to his own imposing height and eased on over to give the little lady a hand, or in this case a foot.

"They got a separate hand pump manned by two choirboys over at Fourteen Holy Martyrs," he confided casually as he calmly sat down beside her to feel for the foot pedals with his longer legs. "You just worry about the fingering of them fine chords and I'll keep the bellows full of air for 'em, ma'am. I answer to the handle of Custis Long and I ride for Marshal Billy Vail as a paid-up lawman, if you're worried about my innocent intentions."

The plump little brunette of about twenty or so favored him

2

with a shy little smile, allowed she was Prunella Farnam, and agreed she'd been having a time reaching the low pedals and high keyboard at once. She proceeded to play far better, and a tad faster, when he started rubbing his right leg against her left one. But there was no way for him to move to his left without hanging half his ass in midair, while she had plenty of room on the rest of the bench if she cared to shift her own.

She didn't seem to want to. Longarm mostly kept his desperately casual gray eyes on the crowd to their left as he stroked away at her and the organ to his right. She seemed to be breathing sort of fast, even though he'd taken over the harder chore, as she played a familiar church tune he didn't know the words to.

Leastways, he didn't know the words they'd doubtless put down on paper to be sung on such solemn occasions. Like many a country boy before him, Longarm had grown up memorizing more scandalous words to otherwise tedious songs sung by tedious elders. He and a freckle-faced kid who'd been killed a few summers later at Malvern Hill had sure enjoyed singing "Massa's in de cold, cold ground" as "Mah ass is in de cold, cold ground" right in front of the gals with the teacher leading. He'd never rightly figured whether the gals had been fooled or not. Gals often giggled while singing whether there was a joke worth laughing at or not.

But the gal next to him wasn't playing the song about some dead slaveholder's funeral. As he pumped away Longarm tried and failed to come up with the right words, or even the title of this one. But all that popped into his head was:

> "While the organ peeled potatoes,
> Lard was rendered by the choir.
> While the sextant wrang the dish cloth,
> Someone set the church on fire!"

The plump brunette bumped his longer, leaner leg with a plump thigh deliberately, as she giggled. "Stop that! This is

3

supposed to be a very solemn occasion and you mustn't make me laugh!"

So he tried not to. But the next thing he knew, as he was biting his own disrespectful tongue, he caught her mouthing the next verse under her breath. So it seemed only fair to sing along:

> "Holy smoke, the preacher shouted.
> In the rush he lost his hair.
> Now his head resembles Heaven,
> For there is no parting there."

She botched a note, poked him with an elbow, and warned him with mock severity that she'd stand him in a corner if he didn't cut that out. Then she switched to another dirge, and Longarm had to stifle a laugh. For the only words he knew to *that* one were from a really filthy parody.

He resisted the impulse, even though he suspected she knew full well how the sillier version went. Young gals had been just as silly as anyone else growing up back home in West-by-God-Virginia.

So he just went on pumping her organ as she inspired his with a calico-covered thigh and the solemn notes of what he only recalled as "Cock of Ages."

Then they had to quit horsing around in the organ alcove for a spell as the preacher and some other professional liars said nice things about the old dead drunk in the fancy box. As he sat there, off to one side with Prunella, Longarm murmured a suggestion as to what they ought to play him out of the church with. She said she'd do it if he promised not to sing the dirty words to "Farther Along."

He assured her, "It's one of my favorite hymns sung straight. Most of 'em promise all sorts of things I ain't so sure they can ever deliver. But that more sensible one only suggests we'll all understand this confusion farther along in the mysterious hereafter."

He shot a somber glance at the raised lid of the old drunk's

4

casket as he thoughtfully added, "Right now, the guest of honor in yonder box knows more about what lies yonder than the rest of us."

"If anybody does," she demurred in a wistful tone. "The poor old man wasn't able to make a lick of sense with his brain full of whiskey. How clear might it function full of embalming fluid?"

Longarm made a wry face and observed that that seemed to be a sort of scientific attitude for a church organist. To which she replied, "I'm here for the same reasons most everyone else was invited. The poor old thing was too important to send off with only the very few who cared about him. They asked me to play this organ because I said I knew a few hymns they didn't have the music for. After I see him out the front door with 'Farther Along' I'm calling it a day here. It looks like rain and the Methodist Burial Grounds on the south side of town are over a mile away."

Longarm sighed. "You're right about the coming rain. It's been a mighty wet greenup so far this year. But my boss, Marshal Vail, lent me his family surrey for the occasion, and it's a good thing we put up the side curtains this morning suspecting that early overcast of soggy intentions."

She shrugged, somehow moving her thigh against his in the process, as she softly replied, "It's too bad you feel obliged to drive out to the burial grounds then. With my luck the hansom I hail out front will have open sides and my skirts will surely get spotted by the time I'm home."

When he hesitated, weighing the odds of his being seriously missed in a crowd of rain-soaked strangers, she threw in, "Fortunately, I don't live far. So no matter how wet I get, I'll doubtless be snug and dry in my Turkish bathrobe, sipping hot chocolate by the fire, by the time the rest of you wade free of that fresh-laid sod out on the south side of town."

Longarm grimaced and quietly asked, "Might you have any toasting spits and marshmallows to go with that rainy-day fire, ma'am?"

She murmured, "My friends call me Pru, and I suppose we

5

could stop along the way for fresh marshmallows if that would be your pleasure."

But it wasn't. So of course they didn't, as he drove her the other way through a serious April shower while everyone else headed out to the south in the wake of that rubber-tired hearse drawn by six black high-steppers. Billy Vail's less imposing surrey only rated a team of ill-matched bays. But Pru said they were sweet, and Longarm thought *she* might be as well when she suggested the horses would be better off rubbed down, fed, and watered in her own carriage house seeing that he might be staying long enough to toast some marshmallows.

He wasn't dumb enough to scout for a grocery shop open on a rainy Sabbath, or remark on her earlier admission that they'd not find any marshmallows once they got to her place on Logan Street. For he'd learned early on that there was nothing a mortal man could do to speed the pace of a woman with her mind made up. On the other hand, a total fool could change a woman's mind and cool her off by clumsy moves or the wrong words. So he hardly said anything as he and Billy Vail's team followed her directions. Sure enough, the next thing he knew the two of them were warming up before the coal fire in her bedchamber with nary a marshmallow or even that Turkish bathrobe to distract them. She did most of the work, on top, with the ruby glow from the coal fire inspiring a man to new heights as it rippled over her voluptuous torso and naked bouncing bubbles.

They naturally finished up in her four-poster across the room, with him on top, and then they shared one of his three-for-a-nickel cheroots with her tousled brown hair spread across his bare chest. He could have found out a lot more about her had he wanted. But he changed the subject to their more recent delights as she began to tell him the story of her life. He'd already figured she lived alone as a grown woman of some property on the fashionable side of Lincoln Street. So after that, anything else she had to tell a new lover figured to be depressing. Most men knew better than to brag about catching the clap off Arapaho squaws who beat them when they came

6

home drunk. So he'd never figured out why gals felt they had to tell every young boy they met about getting screwed in the ass by an elder brother while their mothers beat them with horsewhips. So he assured old Pru he didn't care who'd been in the right or wrong during her recent divorce and property settlement. He put out their smoke, and put what she said she liked better back where she said she liked it best.

He wouldn't know what a mess he was in before he'd spent a good eighteen hours with her, laying, lying, or whatever. As another silly song suggested, if she'd had wings, he'd have screwed her flying!

It would have been rude to take leave of such a swell hostess right after she'd served him ham and eggs in bed even though it *was* a workday. So Longarm got to the Federal Building along about ten, still walking a mite funny. He didn't need the smirking typewriter-player in the front office to tell him what a chewing he was in for. He just sighed and said, "Don't try to understand it, Henry. Maybe someday, once you figure out why boys and girls are built different, you'll get out of the habit of showing up so early every damned old Monday morn!"

The skinny pale-faced clerk assured Longarm he liked women just fine, in moderation, and added, "You'd better get on back there and take your medicine like a man, Custis. Our boss is really pissed at you this time."

Longarm shrugged and strode on back to the oak-paneled private office of Marshal William Vail. He resisted the impulse to cast a guilty glance at the banjo clock on one wall. He sat uninvited in Billy Vail's field of fire and told the shorter, older, and stouter cuss on the far side of that cluttered desk, "Had to make certain your team was warm and dry after I washed down your surrey up in the carriage house at your place, Billy. Got a hell of a lot of 'dobe on the chassis, thanks to all that rain yesterday."

Billy Vail bit down on the stubby cigar in his bulldog mouth and replied, "Bullshit! You never drove that gal out to no graveyard along no dirty roads! You run her straight home from the funeral after carrying on scandalously with her in front of the whole damned congregation!"

Longarm tried, "I was only helping the lady pump the organ, for Pete's sake!"

Vail repressed a chuckle and managed to turn it into a snap as he replied, "Her husband's name is Paul, not Pete. But you sure as thunder did a heap for *his* sake. He's been trying to catch somebody pumping his wife's organs, and what'll you bet he had the two of you followed, and timed, by the detective firm he's had watching her a good six months or more!"

Longarm gulped. "Hold on. Old Pru assured me she was a grass widow, divorced from a jealous brute whose name seemed unimportant to me at the time."

Vail snapped, "You'll get to know him a heap, and vice versa, if we let him serve you with the papers he's likely having drawn up at this very moment. The gal didn't exactly lie to you. She just left out some truth. Prunella and Paul Farnam are *sort* of divorced, as of last month. But it won't be final till the end of ninety days."

Longarm smiled sheepishly. "She did seem anxious to get on with her, ah, new life. I ain't sure I follow your drift about this ninety-day shit, though. She told me the feelings had been mutual and her ex-husband had been a sport about the house and some mining property up to the Front Range."

Vail grimaced. "She meant Paul Farnam has a far slicker lawyer than she hired. Only I see she doesn't know it yet. Farnam figured he might lose a contested divorce, since his wife was far from the only resident of Colorado who considers him to be a total bastard. There's mining camps old Paul can't go to without a four-man bodyguard. So he gets good rates from that detective agency. As I get it from the courthouse gang, he slickered that passionate but dumb brunette by agreeing to an uncontested divorce and handsome property settlement with just one little provision in the small print."

Longarm sighed and said, "You mean they have her word in small print that she won't entertain overnight guests of the male persuasion under their mutual roof until such time as the court decrees she's free?"

Vail nodded. "Something like that. Knowing her nature even better than the rest of us, I'd say he and his lawyer figured she'd never hold out for ninety days. So tell me something about you. Have you ever suffered any serious fevers?"

Longarm blinked, hesitated but a moment, and replied, "Sure I have. Growing up hard-scrabble in West-by-God-Virginia, we sort of felt left out if we weren't served a dose of any ague going round, and there sure was a heap of 'em. Close to half the kids I started in the first grade with died of one damned fever or another, while the rest of us grew up immune to most. Sink or swim was all the medical science most of our folks could afford."

He glanced out the nearest window at the busy world outside as he caught himself muttering, "Old Warts Wilson died at Cold Harbor after living through the pox, and Hank Bronson licked the scarlet fever only to stop a round of .75 with his head at Shiloh. But that's all water under the bridge, and what have childhood agues to do with me getting hauled into divorce court like the fool that I am about frisky women?"

Vail said, "If you're not in town, you can't be served. If Paul Farnam doesn't serve *some* fool in less than ninety days and prove him a carnal correspondent in court within that time, your Prunella is off the hook, and more important, so's my senior deputy. I only wanted to make sure you had a sporting chance against the fevers of the Fever Coast. I got a half-failed mission down yonder, and seeing you're only fixing to get in a bigger mess here in Denver . . ."

"Hold on and back up," Longarm said with a puzzled frown. "I know they call that stretch of the Texican shore from, say, Brownsville to Galveston the Fever Coast because it's sort of lethal to man or beast from other parts. I've been down that way a time or two and I'm still breathing. But how can a mission be *half*-failed, Billy? Seems to me a man ought to carry out his mission all the way or consider it a *total* failure, right?"

9

"Wrong," Billy Vail replied. "I sent Deputy Gilbert down to a seaport called Escondrijo, betwixt Brownsville and Corpus Christi. I sent him to pick up and transport a federal prisoner for Judge Dickerson down the hall. Gilbert got there to find his prisoner too sick to move from his cot in the town lockup. They told him it was a spring fever that seemed to be going round. Up to then a good half of them down with it had bounced back. So Gilbert hired a room across from the jail to wait his prisoner's fever out. Last I heard, the outlaw Judge Dickerson wants to hang has recovered his own health, whilst poor old Rod Gilbert's flat on his back with that same fool fever."

Leaning back in his swivel chair, Billy Vail relit his soggy old cigar. "To tell the truth, I'd planned on letting Gilbert get better and bring his man in before you got your own fool self in this worse fix. But seeing you have, what say we send you down to Escondrijo to see about getting both old boys back up this way in as much comfort as they both deserve?"

Longarm sighed. "I reckon it beats being hauled into a damned old divorce court any time of the year, and it might not be too hot in south Texas this early in the year. I'll just tell Henry out front, and tend me a few errands whilst he types up my travel orders and vouchers, right?"

"Wrong," Billy Vail replied again. "I've already told Henry what I want typed up for you, Gilbert, and your prisoner. I'll get word to Prunella Farnam later and save you the trouble and considerable risk of running back up yonder to warn her they'll be riding hard on her with spiteful intent. It ain't *our* worry if she can't hold out till you can help her with her organ some more when her dad-blamed divorce is final!"

Longarm smiled sheepishly and said, "Well, as long as somebody warns her . . . It sure feels spooky working for a boss who reads my mind so good, Billy Vail."

To which Marshal Vail could only reply with a modest smile, "I reckon somebody has to do some thinking for you when it comes to women. Lord knows the pretty little things surely seem to confuse the shit out of you when left to study about 'em on your own!"

Chapter 2

Longarm spoke enough Border Mex to translate Escondrijo freely as "Hideout." So he wasn't too surprised to discover Escondrijo, Texas, was one of those places you just couldn't get to from most anywhere else without a whole lot of trouble.

The Lone Star and erstwhile Confederate State was commencing to attract more settlers and railroad tracks now that President Hayes had called a halt to Reconstruction and let those who best knew the Southwest run it their own way, as long as they remembered who'd won. So most of the Southern railroads had standardized their tracks to the same broad gauge, and Henry had managed to get Longarm by rail to the head of navigation on the Rio Grande. You had to go by steamboat from Brownsville to Escondrijo and beyond in any case. Railroads ran where there was profit to be made, across sensible terrain, and even if there had been enough settlers to matter, it would have been a bitch to lay track across the line of swamps and estuaries between Brownsville and Galveston with the construction methods of the day. So it made more sense to everyone if such freight and passengers as there were moved up and down the Fever Coast by boat, whether sail luggers out on the gulf, or steamers plying the inland waterway a good pilot could follow from lagoon to lagoon behind the sandy barrier islands that lay just offshore—as if to guard the low, swampy mainland from that mean Indian deity Hura Kan.

Longarm had known better than to head for south Texas in a three-piece tweed suit with summer coming in. The paddle-wheel passage down the lower Rio Grande was hot and sticky enough to a gent wearing no more than a thin cotton work shirt and well-washed jeans between his tobacco-brown Stetson and low-heeled stovepipe boots. Nobody along the border got excited by the sight of a sober gent packing a gun on one hip. He only sported his badge when he was up to answering pesky questions about his immediate intent.

He'd been fooled before about whether a lawman on such a routine mission might or might not need to do some riding. So this time, seeing he needed someplace to pack his possibles in any case, he'd brought along his personal McClellan saddle and army bridle with his roll, saddlebags, and Winchester '73 attached. Henry'd told him there was a Coast Guard station near Escondrijo, and so he'd doubtless be able to borrow a government mount there in the unlikely event he had to ride out after any escaped fever victims.

The paddle-wheel trip down to Brownsville was uneventful. He boarded a larger coastal steamer there without incident, just in time to be on his way north on the next tide just before suppertime, his cabin steward told him. So he tipped the helpful colored gent a generous two bits in hopes his cabin would stay locked, locked his baggage up for the moment, and ambled back out on deck to enjoy some salt air as well as a smoke. He naturally stationed himself to seaward on the shady side of the long promenade deck. His tobacco smoke still felt far cooler than the steamy breeze stirred up by the steamer's steaming at around six knots. There wasn't any shoreward sea breeze at the moment, and six knots of apparent breeze didn't do a lot for a man who'd just come down from the higher and drier climes of Colorado.

Traveling Denver folks often remarked on how thick and soggy the air felt, even on a dry day in, say, Frisco or Saint Lou. Most found San Antone a steam bath as early as April. Folks from that far north in Texas tried to avoid the gulf coast once the robin began to drift north to cooler summer climes.

"Doesn't it ever cool off down here?" a plaintive female voice was bleating from behind him. So Longarm turned with a smile, noting with regret that the willowy ash-blonde in the middy blouse and straw boater hadn't been talking to him at all. Her complaint seemed to be aimed at a pink-faced jasper in a rumpled white merchant marine cap and uniform. Longarm recognized him as the purser he'd had to check in with coming aboard. The poor bastard was sweating like a hog in that choke-collared linen suit as he somehow managed to assure the blond passenger, "Things will cool off a heap once the sun goes down, ma'am. The nights are way cooler along this coast, and as soon as we hit the more open waters of Laguna Madre the skipper will be ordering more speed."

Longarm doubted that. They'd swung north into the Laguna Madre if he was any judge of maps and if the distant shoreline to either side meant spit. But it would have been pointless as well as rude to call a ship's officer a bare-faced liar, or point out how hot and steamy most cabins figured to remain no matter how much steam they fed the twin screws back yonder. These coastal steamers got more cargo space by using the more modern screw drive, but the smaller boilers they could get by with had no more speed to offer. Steamers poking up and down the gulf coast made their money on stopping as often as possible, not by getting anywhere in such an all-fired hurry.

The sun was low, he could tell—not by looking to the west on the sunny side, but by admiring the first evening star in a purple sky to the east. It would still be some time before any evening breeze picked up its lazy heels. But he still drifted forward towards the dining salon as he finished his smoke. For whether traveling by rail or water, a man with a tumbleweed job soon learned to never be first or last to be seated for dinner.

The dining salon was already crowded as Longarm entered from a shady doorway and drifted to an empty table, on the sunny side but near an open window. His brow felt somewhat cooler as he hung up his hat and sat down by the window. The setting sun was still spiteful, but the faint breeze from the bow almost made up for it as a colored waiter, cheerful enough considering his white choke-collar jacket, came over to hand him a menu and fill a tumbler with ice water for him. How a gent used to this climate managed to keep his jacket no more rumpled than the linen tablecloths all around was a total mystery to a man feeling wilted as hell in a thin blue shirt with an open collar.

Longarm was scanning the menu for something that looked safe as well as cooling when that same ash-blonde came over to ask if the seat across from him was taken. She seemed less distressed by his rough costume when he rose to his feet to assure her she was welcome to join him as long as she refrained from sipping the ice water.

As they both sat down, she frowned thoughtfully at his glass and asked what was wrong with sipping ice water on such a hot afternoon. He glanced about to make certain he wasn't insulting any of the help as he softly explained, "There's this French chemist called Pasture, I think, who's been studying on bitty invisible bugs that may spread agues, and they call these waters the Fever Coast with reason, ma'am. I've been down this way before, and I've found it way safer to stick to hard liquor, or hot softer drinks such as tea or coffee. If you order either, make sure you're served stuff too hot to drink right off. Don't order iced desserts or salads down this way either, hear?"

She looked more amused than annoyed as she observed, "Oh, dear, and I was looking foreward to the shrimp salad here. I take it you're some sort of physician, good sir?"

Longarm laughed easily. "Not hardly. I'm a federal deputy marshal. Name's Custis Long. So you go right ahead and order the iced shrimp if you've a mind to, and I'll tell 'em you died brave if you guessed wrong. The odds are better'n eight out of ten in your favor, ma'am. I just don't value the taste of shrimp cocktail that highly, having witnessed a few cases of food poisoning whilst passing through these parts in the past."

The willowy blonde made a wry face—it still remained fair to gaze upon—and decided, "Brrr, I don't think I like those

14

odds myself. So what do you suggest, seeing you seem so familiar with the local cuisine?"

He replied without hesitation, "Anything Mex served hot, ma'am. I know hot tamales or chili con carne washed down with cold rum or hot coffee sounds dumb. But the Mex folk, who've lived down this way longer, hardly ever come down with food poisoning. Hot spicy grub must kill them bitty bugs that French chemist has been studying."

She studied the menu he'd handed her dubiously, telling him that she'd read about Louis Pasteur in a ladies' magazine devoted to female problems and getting the vote. Then she asked if he'd read anything about that other scientist blaming tropical fevers on the bites of bigger bugs, such as flies, ticks, and even mosquitoes.

He nodded. "Him too. You're talking about that Anglo-Cuban doctor, Carlos Finlay, who keeps saying yellow jack and Texas fever might be spread by bug bites. I don't see why they can't both be right. Meanwhile, I see that waiter coming back. So do you trust me to order for the both of us, Miss . . . ?"

"Colbert, Lenore Colbert," she said with a bemused smile. "I suppose I'll have to trust you when it comes to hot tamales and so forth. I've never eaten any Mexican food no matter which of those scientists may be right. I don't see how they could *both* be right, though."

The waiter was there by this time. So Longarm allowed they'd both go for chili con carne, tamales, and chicken enchiladas, knowing most Anglo palates could manage such beginner's fare. He suggested, and she agreed to, black coffee laced with white rum. As the waiter left, Longarm explained, "I don't hold with one cause for all fevers. It only stands to reason that fevers as different as, say, scarlet, yellow, and the ague or chills-and-fever can't be caused by the same whatever. We know now that the milk fever that killed Abe Lincoln's mother was inspired by poisonous snakeroots their milch cow had been into. For some reason the poison passes through the cow harmlessly to kill human folks who drink her milk. But

15

you don't have to drink milk to come down with yellow jack or even the Texas fever northern cows die from. So maybe both Pasture and Carlos Finlay could be on to the truth. Or half the truth leastways. I suspect there's way more to coming down sick than modern medicine has a handle on. I know my own job's more complicated than some figure. I've wound up mighty confounded by two separate crimes I was trying to solve as the work of one outlaw. So what if folks get sick for all sorts of different reasons whilst the docs seek some common cause?"

She was staring past him in a desperately casual manner as she replied, "That's their problem. Don't look now but there's another man boring holes in your back with his cold steel eyes. You *are* on some sort of mission for the government, right?"

Longarm resisted the impulse to turn his head as he smiled at her uncertainly and replied, "I am, but it ain't no secret mission, and it wouldn't do anyone a lick of good if they managed to stop me. My office sent me down this way to pick up an owlhoot rider by the name of Clay Baldwin. He's already been arrested and they've been holding him at Escondrijo for us. He'd still be locked up if someone bored real holes in my back and threw me over the side. My boss would likely send two or three deputies to fetch Baldwin as soon as things got that serious. Might you have a bitty mirror in that bag across your lap, Miss Lenore?"

She said she did and, to her credit, never asked why a grown man might want to borrow such a thing. Meanwhile, the waiter got back with their orders. So it was easy enough for her to slip Longarm the small square mirror amid all the confusion atop their table.

As the waiter poured and laced their coffee and the gal across the way stared thunderstruck at the unfamiliar grub in front of her, Longarm found it easy enough to prop the mirror up against a saltshaker. Sure enough, an ugly galoot was staring mean as hell at him from another nearby table. The lean and hungry face failed to remind Longarm of anyone he was currently after. The stranger sat across from another cuss

16

dressed for south Texas riding. But that didn't mean either had to be mixed up in beef or other produce. For it had been six or eight years since Longarm had been a serious cowhand, and wasn't *he* wearing shirt and jeans in this infernal climate?

The one staring mean at Longarm's back had his slate-gray Texas-creased hat on at the table. The one facing the other way had on a less dramatic Carlsbad with its crown crushed cavalry. Their matching white shirts, worn vestless, might have said they were a couple of Texas Rangers if Longarm had had recent trouble with the recently reorganized and often proddy Rangers. But he was on fair terms with the Ranger captain back in Brownsville, and didn't know if they even had a Ranger station up around Escondrijo.

As in the case of federal deputies, the Texas Rangers worked out of widely spaced headquarters, mostly built near towns of some importance, and only chimed into local matters in other parts when a federal or state offense seemed too big for the local law to cope with. So Longarm doubted there'd be any cases the Rangers would be worried about this side of, say, Corpus Christi.

Escondrijo was on this side of Corpus Christi, and a day's ride away in a straight line from that more important stop. But moving along the Fever Coast by horse took longer, thanks to all the inlets and swamps there were to go around. By an ironic trick of geology, as the post office riders had known before coastal steamers got so common along the inland waterway, a rider could move much faster along the back dunes of Padre Island, an otherwise mighty lonely string bean of white sand and seagull shit the winds and waves had piled a few miles out extending from Corpus Christi Pass all the way south to Matamoros in Old Mexico. They said it was healthier as well as a bit cooler out along the barrier sands. It was too bad nobody had yet come up with any way to make a living off no more than white sandy beaches and sunshine.

"What are these things that look like lengths of broomstick boiled in oil?" the blonde across the table was asking as Longarm tried in vain to make out what sort of hardware

17

the sinister strangers had behind him. He adjusted the mirror as he assured her hot tamales were sort of big hollow noodles made of cornmeal and stuffed with spicy ground meat.

When she asked what kind of meat, he decided she'd feel better if he said it was likely beef. Beef was possible, and some folks felt odd about eating goats, cats, dogs, and such. The idea of all that red pepper in a hot tamale was to assure that the meat was safe to eat as well as impossible to identify by taste.

He knew he'd said the right thing when Lenore took an experimental taste, followed by a bigger bite and a sudden grab for her coffee to put out the fire, then a smaller but more relaxed nibble as she decided it was a tad spicy but good.

He dug into his own chili con carne to look busy, with his back to those jaspers in her mirror as he casually replied, "That's doubtless because we've a Texican chef on board, ma'am. Mex grub is peppered more along the border than anywhere north or south of it. I suspect Mexicans and Texicans are trying to prove something to one another. Left to themselves— say as far off as Durango, Mexico, or Durango, Colorado— cooks pepper just enough to make a dish sort of interesting. Further south in Old Mexico they cook lots of other ways, with bananas, rice, and such. I had a chicken basted with hot bittersweet chocolate down Mexico way one time. Reckon that's what they call an acquired taste and . . . I see that one in the lighter-gray Carlsbad is packing a two-gun *buscadero* rig, with the one gun I can make out from here a nickel-plated Schofield."

She said, "These beans are less spicy. What's a Schofield?"

He explained, "A revolver gun, ma'am. Mostly made by Smith & Wesson, but named after Brevet Colonel George Schofield of that Colored Tenth Cav. The colonel wasn't colored. He was the baby brother of General John M. Schofield, in charge of the U.S. Army Small Arms Board during the Grant Administration. Colonel George was stuck with a gross of Model 3 S&W horse pistols left over from an order for the Russian cavalry. It wouldn't be charitable at this late date to guess what the general got out of the deal. The younger Schofield, stuck with using the bargain six-guns in the field, made some improvements on the originals, rechambering 'em for army ammunition to begin with. So by the time they'd sold the first three thousand remodeled Russian cavalry guns to their own army, they were so delighted they renamed the gun the Schofield."

She was too polite to indicate she was sorry she'd asked. But he knew women would rather talk about clothes and such. Hence he added, more tersely, "Let's just say the Texas Rangers are issued the Colt .45 Peacemaker one at a time. A man packing two Schofields in tie-down holsters is showing off or expecting some serious fighting. Either way, I doubt they could be Rangers, and I'd be likely to recognize any well-known outlaws in these parts."

She suggested, "Maybe the one glaring at you just arrived from other parts. He certainly seems to recognize you!"

He volunteered to just get up and see what the cuss was so sore about if such rude staring was getting on the lady's nerves. But she pleaded, "Please don't! I can't stand public scenes, and it's not as if he's done or said anything wrong to either of us!"

So Longarm just went on eating, and a few minutes later, having started earlier, the two mysterious strangers finished, got up, and sauntered out of sight. But not before Longarm had made certain they were both loaded for bear. Neither looked dumb enough to carry six in the wheel on either hip. But assuming they, like him, preferred the hammer of a six-gun riding on one empty chamber, that still tallied out to twenty rounds for them and five for him in the first exchange. He'd left the derringer he usually carried in a vest pocket with his other possibles back in his stateroom. So maybe it was just as well he hadn't yelled at them over their dessert.

By the time he and the willowy blonde were having their own, a raisin pie fresh from the oven, the sun was setting in full glory and he'd learned she was a Boston gal headed home after attending the reading of a distant relative's will back in

Brownsville. She said she meant to get off their coastal steamer and catch herself a train at Houston once they got there.

He didn't feel up to going into the details of moving between the offshore stop at Galveston and the inland rail yards of Houston. He tried not to sound wistful as he said, "I'll only be spending the one night ahead aboard this slow but steady tub if I'm lucky. Might get in in the wee small hours if the skipper keeps his word about putting on some speed."

She sipped the last of her coffee, her hair glowing as pretty as old gold in the fading light from her left as she replied she was sure they'd have been moving faster by this time had the skipper really cared about getting anywhere in a hurry. She added, "At least I booked a stateroom on the seaward side this time. I almost steamed myself to clam chowder coming down this coast a week ago."

He didn't say anything. But it was a good thing he wasn't playing poker with such a keen-eyed gal. For she demanded, "What did I say wrong, ah, Custis? Don't you think I should have booked myself a stateroom on the cooler side?"

To which he could only reply, since she'd asked, "If seaward was the cooler side, Miss Lenore. Winds blow from where it's cooler to where it's warmer. Come daybreak the sunbaked plains to our west will send hot air rising to suck in cooler air off the gulf to our east. But the gulf ain't all that cool as seawater goes. So once the plains cool off a tad under starlight, the warmer waters of the gulf ought to suck land breezes out to sea through such portholes as might be open on the landward side."

The Eastern gal stared across at him like a blue-eyed owl as she insisted, "But I *was* on that side, coming down the coast just a week ago, and as I said, I got steamed like a clam baked in seaweed!"

He chuckled at the memory of some clams he'd had that way the time he'd spent back East on Long Island with another blonde. He said, "I never told you the landward staterooms would be cool. I only meant they wouldn't be as hot and stuffy as the ones catching no breezes at all. You don't have to answer if you find this too indelicate, ma'am. But may I take it you were trying to sleep in a steamer stateroom this far south, at this time of the year, in, ah, modest attire?"

She blinked and said, "Well, of course I had my nightdress on, if that's what you mean! Would you have a lady retire under her sheets as bare as some sort of tropical savage?"

He managed not to grin too knowingly as he quietly replied, "I ain't sure how savage the old-time Coahuiltic were when they still owned this part of Texas, ma'am. But their Mex descendants don't retire under a sheet or anything else when it gets this hot. Seeing I'll be getting off come morning, I'd be proud to let you sleep in my stateroom instead."

He could tell, even by such poor light, how hard she blushed as she gasped, "You really *are* in a hurry, aren't you!"

He had to laugh. Before she could spring up and flounce out he quickly explained. "I only meant I was willing to swap with you for just this one night! I ain't that subtle when I ask a supper companion right out to let me call her sweetheart."

It was her turn to smile, sort of dirty, as she said, "I'm sorry, Custis. I know you've behaved in a perfectly proper way since I first sat down here. Could it have really been less than two hours? How could I feel I've known you such a long while?"

He said, "Time drags out here on the water with nothing but one another to bother knowing. Meeting at sundown helped some. We've shared sunshine and shadow as well as plenty of grub and rum-laced coffee."

She smiled archly. "I'd better not have any more rum if you're to remember me as a lady who keeps her clothes on after dark."

Then she caught herself, blushed again, and softly said, "Oh, I must have had more rum than I thought. I didn't meant to tease like that, Custis. I'm really not the sort of girl who takes anything off in mixed company. But I suppose you knew all the time I was just a flirty old maid, didn't you?"

He assured her, "I've been teased worse, and you ain't old enough to be ashamed of being a maid, if we both mean maid

21

as a gal who's still innocent. Being innocent is what lots of gals brag about, at least to the age of twenty-nine or so."

She looked away and murmured, "I'll be twenty-six this August, and I'm not sure I'm still bragging. But I can't help the way I was brought up, Custis. So unless the man I've been saving myself for comes along, I suppose I'll just wind up like that poor old Olivia Lee in the Congregational burial ground back home."

He had to allow he'd never heard tell of Miss Olivia Lee.

Lenore sighed. "I never knew her either. She died a long time ago. Her headstone reads, 'Here lies Olivia Lee, who died a virgin at ninety-three, God rest her poor soul!' "

Longarm didn't laugh. He didn't think such a fate was funny. But he didn't want the responsibilities that would surely go with busting any twenty-five-year-old cherry so far from home either. So he asked whether she wanted to swap staterooms or not, and once she said she could sure do with an even slightly cooler upper berth, he suggested they get busy with their baggage.

They did. Passengers signed for food and drink and settled with the purser before getting off. But Longarm still left some coins on the table to make up for their longer than usual stay there.

He escorted her to her stateroom first. She was traveling light for a gal who slept with duds on. So he needed no help with her two bags, and never sent for any. He led the way along a corridor running abeam from starboard to port, and put her bags on the floor inside his own cabin. Then he lifted his saddle from the bottom berth, saying, "I'll just tote this load over to your stateroom and we'll both be set. Would you like me to straighten out the purser about the switch, or would you rather thrash it out with him seeing as you'll be staying aboard long after I've gotten off and nobody will be likely to say anything dumb?"

She suggested whichever of them saw the purser first ought to work it out with the steamer line. He agreed that made sense, and backed out the narrow doorway to shift the weight of his heavily laden army saddle higher on his free hip. She came out after him, as if to keep him from getting lost on the way back to her old quarters. It would have sounded dumb, as well as rude, to tell her no girls were allowed. So he never did, and in no time at all his possibles were safely locked away, thanks to their swapping keys. Then the two of them were alone on the starboard promenade deck, staring seaward at the rising moon as they leaned against the rail together. He wanted to kiss her so bad he could taste it. But he didn't. He knew that once they got to swapping spit there'd be no reining in till he found out whether he might or might not go farther. Either way, somebody was likely to get hurt more than finding out would be worth. For Longarm knew all too well how good it could get with a pretty lady suffering from a case of pent-up passion, and even a pretty gal that just lay there had pissing beat by at least a furlong. But one night of love with the Queen of Sheba, played by the lovely Miss Ellen Terry, fresh from a perfumed bath, couldn't make up for that hurt look a man saw in the eyes of a gal he was really letting down.

So he softly suggested, "Land breeze ought to be fixing to start over on the port side, ma'am. Why don't I carry you back to my old stateroom before I go see whether those two you spotted at supper are packing two guns apiece for any sensible reason."

She tilted her face up to his in the moonlight, softly asking, "Isn't there anything else you'd rather do than fight, Custis?"

To which he could only reply, "There's plenty, starting with just minding my own beeswax, Miss Lenore. But they don't pay me to avoid fights, and like you said yourself, that one jasper in the big hat surely seems to be spoiling for one!"

Chapter 3

The combined smoking salon and taproom lay aft of the sleeping quarters for sensible reasons. There was no sign stating women were not allowed. But it was generally understood by the traveling public that such dimly lit and smoke-filled areas were not intended for the giggles of females or the patter of little feet. There was a ladies' salon up forward for that.

Longarm was glad. He'd pinned on his federal badge and unsnapped his pocket derringer from the more dangerous end of his watch chain, and had the sneaky two-shot .44 palmed in his big right fist as he came through the starboard entrance. His bigger .44-40 double-action was there for the world to see on his left hip, plain but hand-fitted grip forward, so he could draw as well sitting down, standing up, or astride.

The two he was looking for were across the salon against the bar. They both stood with their backs to the bar, as if they might have been expecting someone. Now that he could see the face of the one in the Carlsbad hat, he could see it was no improvement on the ugly mutt wearing the darker Texas hat, although that was still the one with the meanest expression. They were both heeled with double rigs, worn too low for trouble on horseback but just right for a stand-up showdown.

Longarm strode right over to them as, off to his left, an older gent dealing cards at a corner table muttered, "Oh, shit, I reckon we'll play this hand later, boys. This child is going out on deck for some fresh air and he strongly advises you all to follow!"

Longarm didn't worry about the action that followed to either side as he simply stopped two paces from the bar and casually but firmly stated, "I'd be Custis Long and I'm the law, federal. One of the nicer things about my job is that I don't have to shilly-shally with suspicious characters. So I'd like you gents to state your own names and tell me why you've been acting so suspicious."

As he'd hoped, they'd been braced for the usual bullshit involving narrow-eyed stares and veiled remarks leading up to what they had in mind. So they both froze as each waited for the other to say the first words or make the first move.

In the meantime both kept their hands politely clear of their four guns. So Longarm demanded, "Cat's got your tongues?"

The mean-eyed one in the bigger hat stared back even meaner as he came unstuck and croaked, "We know who you are, Longarm. Neither one of us is wanted by any federal court in the land."

Longarm said, "I already figured as much. Had either of you fit any wanted fliers I've read recently, I'd have come in with my side arm drawn. I don't shit around like those lawmen in Ned Buntline's wild and woolly magazines. I'm asking you once more to state your names and business. It's all the same to me whether you'd care to do as I say or fill your fists."

Somebody else tore out a side door as the more sensible-looking one in the paler hat gulped and protested, "Hold on, Longarm. You can't just throw down on law-abiding citizens for no good reason!"

Longarm insisted, "You're giving me good reason. The law gives me the right to ask anyone this side of President Hayes to state his name and business, and the right to arrest and hold him on suspicion for seventy-two hours maximum should he give me probable cause. As for whether you want to come quiet or shoot it out right here and now, I'm assuming anyone who tells a federal law-man to just go fuck himself isn't planning on coming quiet."

The one in the Carlsbad hat said quickly, "I'd be Hamp Godwynn and this would be Saul Reynolds, better known as

Squint Reynolds for reasons you can see for your own self. We are poor but honest cowhands in search of honest employment."

"Aboard a coastal steamer, acting suspicious and packing two guns apiece in border bully rigs?"

The one called Squint replied, in a surprisingly boyish tenor, "It was border bullies we got armed against. We were just down this way to see if we could get hired on at that monstrous ranch some steamboat skipper started at the mouth of the Rio Grande. We found they mostly hired Mex buckaroos, the cheap bastards."

Longarm smiled thinly. "I reckon you mean *vaqueros*, and I know the big spread you just mentioned. Since I've no good reason to call any grown man here a liar, I'll only say you could've saved us all some needless sweat on a hot night by simply answering me sensibly in the first place. Now that we all know who's talking to whom, let's talk about all them dirty looks you boys were aiming my way earlier this evening at supper up forward."

Hamp Godwynn said, "Squint wasn't aiming dirty looks at you in particular, Longarm. He looks that mean-eyed at everybody, and I don't mind telling you we've had this conversation with other gents who took Squint's natural expression wrong."

Longarm considered, shrugged, and said, "We've all been out with a gal whose naturally flirty eyes drew unexpected as well as unwelcome attentions from others. But like I told one version of that flirty gal on one occasion, there's no need to back up a naturally troublesome expression with a chip on one's cold shoulder."

Squint Reynolds snapped, "We told you who we was and said we was sorry about scaring you. What more do you want, an egg in your beer?"

Longarm answered, firmly but not unkindly, "For your information, I ain't scared of you and your kin combined. But since you've given me information I can check out later, we'll just say no more about it for now. I'd offer to buy a round if

I liked either one of you and it wasn't so blamed stuffy in here. But since I don't and it ain't, I'll just say *buenoches* and don't go glaring like that no more if we should meet at breakfast, hear?"

Then he left. He didn't have to crawfish backwards. There was a big glass window offering him a good view of everyone in the salon as he strode out to the starboard promenade deck.

Once he had, it didn't feel much cooler. But the promenade deck got its name because it went all the way round the upper passenger section of the combined freight and passenger steamer from stem to stern.

He was closer to the stern at the moment. So he got out a cheroot and lit it in the still-muggy air on that side. Then he ambled aft and rounded the last stern corner to discover that, just as he'd told pretty Lenore, a fairly strong land breeze was blowing from the west. It smelled of mesquite and was far from frigid. But at least it was dry and brisk enough to cool his face and sweat-soaked shirt as he strolled forward along the deserted portside deck. The staterooms he passed were built back to back, save for the few facing a companionway or warped into odder shapes by funnels, airshafts, and ladderways. So most of them opened out to the promenade deck with ventilation jalousies built into lower door panels as well as their port shutters. That was what they called windows on a boat, whether they looked like portholes or not. So you could hear things going on inside as you passed many a stateroom, most by this time dark. Victorian folks didn't go to sleep with the chickens because of religious notions. Oil lamps gave off a lot of heat as they shed piss-poor light for reading. Hence, as in the case of the chickens, most Anglo-Americans of the era were early to bed and early to rise simply so they could see what they were doing. The Mexican folks on both sides of the border were the night owls. Not as many were interested in reading, and after that it was just too hot down this way during Yanqui business hours. So the "lazy Mex" broke his day up into short hard stints from the wee small hours to

27

the heat of late morning, dozed off in the shade most of the afternoon, and often put in another eight or ten hours of work or play in the cool shades of evening.

Lenore Colbert had already told him she was a Yanqui gal. So he wasn't surprised to see she'd trimmed her lamp and likely turned in by the time he passed his old stateroom. He was tempted to pause for a few puffs on his smoke and see if he could hear her snoring, jerking off in bed, or whatever. But he never did. It made a man wistful enough to picture a pretty gal alone in bed, either decorous under the sheets, or spread-eagled atop them buck naked.

He could guess how the couple two staterooms up were most likely dressed for bed as he passed their dark shutters and heard a female voice cry out, "Ooh, that feels wicked and I know I'll surely burn in Hades when I die, but right now I want your tongue even deeper!"

Longarm chuckled silently and moved on, muttering, "Aw, with any luck all those French saints will put in a good word for you, ma'am. Those French are a caution for eating pussy and turning into saints, and there's nothing about that in the Ten Commandments to begin with. The sinners in Sodom wanted to screw boy angels in the ass. I never read what the folk in Gomorrah, Admah, and Zeboiim were up to. The Good Book just don't say. But it must have been worse than they do in Dodge when the herds are in town because Dodge and even Frisco are still there, praise the Lord."

Others along the way seemed to be just screwing, snoring, or in one case arguing in bed about whether they could afford a new carpet in the front parlor. Then he passed the dining salon, shut for the night, and finally he was standing alone in the bows, where the combined air movements made him feel so good he wondered why nobody else was standing there with him. Then, reflecting on the night watch above him on the Texas deck, the black gang down below in the engine room, and most of the folks in the staterooms being the type to call ports on a steamer windows, he realized it only stood to reason a more experienced traveler would get to hog such comfort as there was aboard this tub on such a muggy night.

He finished his smoke, tossed the lit stub over the side to admire its firefly dive to the inky gulf waters, and resisted the temptation to light another. He'd been trying to cut down on tobacco. For some reason he found it tougher than refusing another drink after his legs warned him he'd had enough, or leaving a gal's skirts alone after she'd warned him she was married or, even more dangerous, a maiden pure. Yet anyone could see a man got more pleasure out of strong liquor or weak-willed women than tobacco had ever offered. So why in tarnation did a man on such a modest salary have to spend a whole nickel to smoke only three damned cheroots that neither made him feel like singing or coming?

On the other hand, he was already uncomfortable enough as he leaned on the rail in sweaty duds with half a hard-on. So he lit up some more, muttering, "Just this last one before we turn in for at least a few hours' sleep. Don't want folks thinking a drunk might be coming down the gangplank at 'em come morning."

As anyone who's ever tried to cut down on smoking knows, a smoke seems to burn down faster as soon as you tell it you don't mean to have another in the near future. So maybe a quarter hour later he watched that one diving to the sea as he reached absently for a third, another part of him pointing out, "What the hell, may as well spend the whole nickel before we turn in."

But he shook his head firmly and told himself, "A man's word is a man's word. Who in Creation is a man supposed to trust if he breaks his damned word to his damned self?"

He toughed it out another ten minutes or so, then found himself on the move again, aimed for Lenore's starboard stateroom but drifting back along the port side, to windward, if only to postpone the stagnant heat to seaward by taking the long route round the stern.

The moon was shining on the far side. So Longarm moved aft along the darker deck as no more than an inky blur, thanks to passing on that third smoke. Hence they didn't spot him either as they kicked in a stateroom door further down and charged in shooting.

Longarm drew his own side arm and advanced on the confusion, getting there just as two dark blurs were backing out of his original stateroom through their own cloud of gunsmoke. So he demanded they freeze and fired almost in the same moment when neither did. He hit the nearest one and suspected he knew who it was as his target dropped faster than its big hat. He put another round in the son of a bitch before pegging his fifth and last shot at the sound of the other one's thudding boot heels. Then he crouched just inside the open doorway, reloading six in the wheel as he bawled loudly, "Everybody stay put inside in the name of the law!"

Then he asked more softly, "Are you all right, Miss Lenore?"

He got no reply as he sprang back up to chase after the one called Godwynn. Halfway back to the stern he heard a mighty splash, and nobody seemed on deck ahead of him as he rounded the last corner. So he swung back to peer back along the barely visible wake in the moonlight, muttering, "I hope there's plenty of sharks trailing this vessel if that was you I just heard, you bastard!"

By the time he got back to his shot-up stateroom the smoke had cleared and there were others out on deck despite his command to stay inside their rooms. He recognized the white uniform of the purser in the dim light and called out, "Deputy Long here. I reckon you noticed that gunplay just now. I'd be obliged if you'd have a look at the one on the deck betwixt us whilst I see about somebody nicer I was trying to do a favor for!"

He struck a match as he stepped inside. The small space still reeked of the brimstone breath of six-guns. He lit a wall fixture, and felt sorry he'd done so as he saw what lay atop the sheets of the upper berth. Lenore Colbert had taken his advice about flopping buck naked in such ventilation as might get through those jalousies near the head of the berth. So you could see every bullet hole in her willowy naked body, and they'd sure put enough in her. But she was bleeding too much

30

to be sincerely dead. So he holstered his gun to move over to her, snatching up some bedding to rip into white bandages as he wondered, heartsick, where to start.

She was bleeding hardest from a wound under one shapely breast. He shoved a twist of cotton sheeting into it before he commenced an attempt to wrap a longer strip around her chest. A gal that skinny lifted easy and he tried to move her gently. But she moaned and said, "You're hurting me. What happened? Is that you, Custis?"

He said, "It is. You've been shot. I got one of 'em and it looks as if the other one dove overboard. Hold still and let me knot this dressing secure till we can find you a sawbones."

She protested, "Oh, Lord, I don't have any clothes on. Please trim that lamp. I can't have you seeing me naked!"

He said, "Already have, and I'm sure glad to see you've neither tattoos nor a tail, ma'am. I reckon that'll hold your left lung in you for now. Let's see about this other round you took under your floating rib."

"Don't look at my privates!" she pleaded as he removed his hat and gently covered her blond pubic hair with it while refraining from telling her he already had. It might have upset her as much to be told no man with a lick of sense had horny thoughts about even a great naked body shot so full of lead.

The purser came in, gasped in dismay at the sight of the bloody nude on the upper berth, and recovered to soberly state, "Our Mister Reynolds outside is beyond any need for medical attention. But I sent for the ship's surgeon in any case. Is the lady still alive and may one ask what she was doing in your stateroom if you weren't in here with her, Deputy Long?"

Longarm said, "For now let's say we swapped berths because she was suffering more than me from your great weather down this way. I got a better question. How did those two killers learn which stateroom I was supposed to be holed up in tonight?"

The purser sighed. "I told them. They were asking about you in the smoking salon a few minutes ago. I allowed that since I'd not seen you on deck and there was nothing else open you were likely in bed. The other one, Mister Godwynn, said he wanted to slip a note under your door and he seemed so friendly . . ."

"I follow your drift," Longarm snapped. "Now I'd like you to round up some armed and dangerous crewmen and make sure that was Godwynn I just heard going over the taffrail. I chased him as far as the stern and lost him one way or the other."

The purser stated flatly, "If he went over the side he's done for. We're miles off either shore in a shark-infested lagoon. Even in the unlikely event he might make it ashore, there's nothing there if you get there!"

Longarm said, "I know Padre Island is a desert island with nothing to eat or a drop to drink for farther than any man could hope to walk in this climate. Tell me more about the mainland over to our west."

The purser thought and shrugged. "Not a whole lot for a man on foot and probably unarmed by now, even if he was serious about swimming that far. The marshy shores rise to soggy cattle country. A lot more salt grass than cows can eat, away from the rarer fresh water. His only hope, should he make it that way, would be if he could at least find some shade before high noon. Wherever the soil rises high enough above sea level you're likely to find squatters of the Mex or Indian persuasion, if your luck holds out. Anglo squatters along the coast this far from anywhere are more likely to be outlaws who'd kill a man for his boots!"

Longarm finished knotting the bandage around Lenore's trim bare waist and growled, "That Godwynn rascal is an outlaw in his own right. So why are you still standing there? Didn't you just hear me tell you to find out which way he went?"

The purser left. Longarm was trying to figure out what needed bandaging next, and how, when Lenore opened her eyes again and said in a conversational tone, "I'm dying, Custis."

He tried to keep his own voice as calm as he told her, "No, you ain't. You're too pretty and we won't let you."

She sighed and said, "I know I'm pretty, and here I lie, naked as a jay with a handsome man, and I'm still fixing to

32

die a goddamn virgin like poor old Olivia Lee back home!"

He removed his hat from her privates to replace it with a numb but friendly palm, not really feeling anything as he told her, "I just now told you there'd be no dying around here, virgin or not. There'll surely be a Coast Guard dispensary when we get to Escondrijo in just a few hours, and then they'll fix you up so's I can make sure you'll never in this world die a virgin, hear?"

She smiled wanly and softly asked, "Are you threatening to seduce me while I'm helpless, you great-looking brute?"

He chuckled fondly. "Nope. Only when you're well enough to get on top. For once you can, I mean to come in your sweet flesh till all our bones ache."

He was suddenly aware they had company as the dying girl smiled radiantly up at him, or maybe through him, to say, "Why, Custis, that was the nicest thing any man's ever said to me!"

Then she was dead. The white-clad figure that moved around him to feel Lenore's throat looked more like a nurse than any ship's surgeon. Longarm gulped and said, "I know what you just heard must have sounded disgusting, ma'am, but . . ."

"I know what you were trying to do," the plump and motherly gal said. "Few men would know how to be that comforting to a dying woman. It was very gallant of you, Deputy Long."

Chapter 4

Longarm had lived through a war or more. So unlike some
peace officers, he was inclined to let less-than-lethal confusion
simply pile up while he tried to grasp the overall pattern and
watch for snipers. So as soon as the ship's surgeon, red-eyed
and three sheets to the wind, joined them in his stateroom,
Longarm left the dead Lenore to a drunk who couldn't hurt her
and that nursing sister or whatever as he joined the search for
her surviving killer—if the son of a bitch was still on board.

The purser led Longarm down to the cargo deck, where
an officer had his deckhands poking about with bull's-eye
lanterns. The officer was called a supercargo because he supervised the cargo, the way the purser supervised the passengers.

The partly open-sided cargo deck, like those of most coastal
steamers and all riverboats, lay just above the waterline over
the hollow-egg-crate construction of the shallow-draft hull. The
supercargo said they'd already swept the mostly empty barn-
like space. Longarm wanted to make certain, having found a
life preserver missing. Longarm's first impression of the bulkhead further aft was that the steamer's boilers and machinery
lay just beyond. But as the supercargo's gang went through the
motions forward, Longarm paced from port to starboard and
saw he was right about that companionway near his stateroom
being longer. So he rejoined the gruff and somewhat older
supercargo and said, "As big as this open cargo deck may seem,
this vessel gets wider back behind that bulkhead, meaning you

got more than half this level all filled up with coal bins and machinery?"

The supercargo shook his head, billed cap and all. "We've already checked the coal bins, and there's no way he could have gotten into the boiler room or engine compartment without the black gang noticing. There's not as much space for him to work with aft as you seem to imagine. Less than a third of this level holds anything besides cargo. More than a quarter of our length, beyond that bulkhead, is cold storage. We have what amounts to a swamping ice house, refrigerated with those newfangled ammonia and brine pipes. Didn't you know we picked up lots of fresh meat and produce along the way that would never make it to New Orleans or even Galveston in this heat without spoiling?"

Longarm said, "I do now. How do you get inside with, say, a lantern as well as a six-gun?"

The supercargo looked surprised, but pointed at a sort of icebox door off to one side. "That's the only inspection port at this end. Cargo's loaded into the refrigerated hold from the side, from the docks. So there's no way he could have—"

"You just said that smaller entrance allowed an inspector to get through," Longarm noted. "I'd surely be obliged if someone would lend me a lantern and show me how to open that latch. I got my own gun."

The supercargo insisted, even as he was leading the way over with his bull's-eye beam on the oaken port and its stout brass fittings, "Nobody could hide in there with the half-frozen fruit and crates of salad greens we've already cooled to just above zero centigrade."

Longarm shrugged and said, "I've been in colder places, in just my shirtsleeves, and it never killed me. Zero centigrade is a lot hotter than zero Fahrenheit. How come you keep your cold-storage cargo just above freezing?"

The supercargo handed Longarm his lantern. "Hold the beam on the latch while I unlock her, will you? If you freeze meat or produce all the way, the ice needles forming inside turn it all mushy and sooty-looking as it thaws. But ice don't form and stuff don't rot too much just above the freezing point of water."

Longarm nodded. "Some railroad men told me about freeze burn. For now I'm more interested in that fucking Hamp Godwynn, if that was his name."

The supercargo opened the port and let Longarm go ahead with the bull's-eye beam and six-gun as he observed, "We found no certain identification for either when we searched the stateroom they were sharing. They'd told the purser they were cattlemen. Their baggage neither proved it nor made liars out of them. They'd brought along stock saddles with their personal baggage lashed to them."

Longarm swept the beam ahead through the clearing fog stirred up by their entrance along with a blast of warm air. The mostly empty space was about the size of a dance hall, although with a far lower ceiling, but he'd never been to a dance where they had ice-frosted pipes running the length of the two longer walls. He didn't ask a dumb question about the ice on the refrigeration pipes. He knew the air next to ice could be somewhat warmer than freezing. The air in a plain old icebox felt about this cold. It was already raising a gooseflesh under Longarm's shirt as he asked the supercargo what sort of stock saddles they were talking about.

The seagoing Texican replied, "One was a Panhandle double rig, and the other was one of them Mex ropers with the exposed wooden swells and dally horn. You're talking to a man who loads a heap of *beef* along his weary way."

Longarm swept the beam up at the long rows of empty meat hooks as he thoughtfully mused, "They told me they were from other parts and just looking for work down by the border. They both packed their guns in border *buscadero* rigs as well. I sure wish folks wouldn't lie to the law so much."

He aimed his gun at some produce crates further back as he moved in on them, the supercargo trailing with his own gun out. But they only found citrus fruit and a fancy breed of salad greens for the New Orleans French-style of cooking back there. When Longarm asked, the supercargo explained that the little they had aboard up to now came from the Mexican farms around the mouth of the Rio Grande. He said the state and federal health authorities made such a fuss over meat out of Mexico, or anywhere near it, that the shipping company didn't want the bother.

Longarm said he'd heard about the current outbreak of hoof-and-mouth down Mexico way. "You were right about Hamp Godwynn not being refrigerated too. Let's get out of here before we almost freeze our own asses to zero centigrade!"

They ducked back outside. It was the first time since he'd been south of the Texas line that he welcomed the muggy heat of the gulf.

On the way back topside the supercargo admitted they hadn't been able to search any other staterooms because the rest of the passengers had retired for the night.

Longarm said they'd see about that, and proceeded to knock politely but firmly on doors. They found, as he'd hoped, that most law-abiding folks with nothing to hide but their privates were willing to let the law have a look around as long as they got to cover their privates first. The only couple who flatly refused to let Longarm in without a search warrant were the Hades-bound honeymooners he'd heard earlier. Longarm decided not to bend the U.S. Constitution all out of shape just to see what the woman looked like. It was almost bound to be a disappointment, and it was tough to picture them letting Godwynn in to watch.

The son of a bitch wasn't anywhere else on board that Longarm could come up with. So he drifted back to his own stateroom to see how they were doing with poor Lenore.

They'd done better than he'd expected. Somebody had stripped the ruined bloody bedding off the top berth, and the dead blonde was now reposing on the bar springs. That only seemed cruel till you noticed how someone had washed her off, smoothed her hair, and struggled her into a modest ivory flannel nightgown from her own baggage. Longarm felt sure the motherly nurse or whatever had done most of the work, although the boozy ship's surgeon was the one going on about how his company would wire home for her at the next port of call, and then carry her on to the end of the line on ice so someone of her own could meet or have the body met with there.

The motherly gal, a bit older and fatter than Longarm, said she'd drained such blood as those bullets had left in the dead gal and emptied her basin over the rail just outside. That was the first Longarm had noticed, in the soft lantern light, how someone had used face powder and rouge to keep Lenore's face from going that pallid beeswax shade dead faces got before they turned really funny colors. When Longarm asked where she'd learned so much about undertaking, she explained she'd been a Union army nurse in the war. She looked away as she added, "Making them look presentable before their dear ones saw them was the least we could do. Lord knows there was neither the medicine nor the medical skills to save a third of them."

He didn't say he'd been there. He wasn't being modest. He didn't want to remind her how long ago it had been. He was now in his thirties, and he'd had to lie about his age to be allowed to act so foolish. She'd have had to have been in her twenties and able to prove her good character and nursing skills to Sister Clara Barton, the boss of all the Union nurses, before they'd have let her put rouge on dead soldiers-blue. So he figured her for her early forties, give or take hard work and a healthy appetite.

They didn't talk more about the past till after some crewmen had come with an improvised pine coffin to carry poor Lenore down to the cold-storage hold. He told the purser not to bother making up the berth that night. He explained he was getting off in the morning to begin with and already had his own possibles in that other stateroom on the starboard side.

When he told the older army nurse he had a fifth of Maryland rye among those possibles, she dimpled at him and replied, "Lord love you, I could use a stiff drink, and we used to get Maryland rye fresh from the still when I was serving in that charnel house outside of Washington. But lest you feel you've wasted good whiskey, young sir, it's only fair to warn you I don't want anyone making all my bones ache."

Longarm smiled sheepishly and insisted, "I thought we'd agreed I was only trying to comfort a shot-up lady, ma'am. For the record and a lady's reputation, I never even kissed Miss Lenore. All that mush you may have misread sprang from an earlier conversation about a far older lady who died purer than she might have wanted."

The nurse said in that case she'd trust him for just one nightcap in his stateroom. They'd both figured out who he was by now. But along the way to the starboard side she surprised him a tad by introducing herself as Norma Richards, M.D.

He waited until they were in his stateroom with the lamp lit and door wide open before he casually asked, while pouring a tumbler to be shared, whether that wasn't a government nursing uniform she had on. She nodded, took a manly belt from the tumbler, and handed it to him. "It is. I put on my summer whites as soon as I saw how slow we were steaming. I put myself through medical school after the war. I knew I'd done almost nothing for those dying boys. Once I had my own M.D. degree I felt even less respect for some of the army surgeons I'd served under. I'm a good doctor. I don't usually drink this much and I'm interested in medicine. But since we both work for the same government, do I really have to go into why they'd only have me a lab technician with a nurse's rating?"

Longarm sipped some rye and gently replied, "We don't have many female deputies riding out of the Denver District Court, now that you mention it, Miss Norma. About the best a lady can do with our Justice Department is stenographer or prison matron. But I'll bet you're a good lab technician. I saw how slick you tidied up that poor Miss Lenore."

She shrugged and said, "Thank you, I think. I'm damned good. My specialty is bacteriology. It's a whole new science. We didn't know anything about disease germs during the war, and when I think of those poor boys shot full of holes in filthy uniforms and our primitive attempts to irrigate their wounds with pond water I . . . Could I have another drink? I don't know why that girl's death tonight got me so upset. I never knew her and I've seen so much worse in my time."

Longarm poured her a stiffer one as he said soothingly, "You'd have liked her had you known her, and like you said, it's been a while and you've a better notion what's been busted up inside. I've read about germs. I take it you don't treat gunshot wounds any more?"

She sipped some rye, shook her head, and explained. "Despite my womanly rank they have me supervising the setting up of new bacterial departments at army, navy, and Indian agency clinics down this way. I just finished teaching some hairy-chested male physicians down in Brownsville how to use a microscope properly. Ninety-nine percent of what you see wriggling in dirty ditch water seems to do nothing much at all. Some few one-celled microbes are now known to be helpful in baking bread and turning malted rye to gold, like we're drinking. A few others are really bad bugs. The ones causing the cholera look a bit like tadpoles. The ones that may cause the ague, or malaria, seem to look like either wriggle worms or doughnuts. They both show up in the blood of ague victims, and laugh if you like, I have my own theory they're two stages of the same organism. But when I sent in a paper to the *Medical Journal* they sent it back. They were too polite to call me a hysterical woman."

Longarm moved over to the doorway as he soberly replied, "I reckon if a catty-pillar could turn into a butterfly, a wriggle worm ought to manage turning into a doughnut, ma'am. But to tell the truth, I doubt anyone aboard this vessel died of the ague this evening."

There didn't seem to be anyone about outside, but you never knew for certain. So he shut the door before he moved back her way, saying, "I'm sure you're a swell doctor, Miss Norma, but right now I've other favors to ask of you, seeing we both work for the same government and all."

She put the empty tumbler aside on a corner washstand, regarding him with some alarm. "I haven't had *that* much to drink and I told you I didn't want to get on top, cowboy!"

Longarm chuckled. "Well, it's too blamed *hot* for *me* to consider doing all the work. But I wish you'd listen to my proposition before you cloud up and rain all over such a harmless cuss!"

So she listened, and he told her how he thought the two of them, working together, might turn the tables on a killer who had Longarm in a double bind.

As she hesitated, he insisted, "If he made it ashore my only hope is to wire up and down the coast for some posse riders as soon as I can. But if he's somehow managed to hole up aboard this big old tub with all its nooks and crannies . . ."

"I'll do as you ask," she said with a sigh. "So pour me another drink before I change my mind. All in all, I'd rather get on top!"

They got into the sleepy port of Escondrijo by the gray if not really cold light of a gulf coast dawn. Few passengers were up at such an ungodly hour, and those who came out on deck to see what all the fuss was about were told not to go ashore unless, like Deputy Long, they intended to stay there until another coastal vessel put in. For this one was only staying long enough to take on some fresh beef from the one slaughterhouse in town, and save for the few crewmen putting a modest amount of cargo ashore, with Longarm's saddle perched atop a chest of drawers from Old Mexico, the whole crew seemed anxious to pitch in and wrestle the heavy sides of beef up the gangplank leading into the cold-storage hold. So it took less than an hour, and then they were on their way as the sun came up to shed more heat as well as light on things.

The next few hours passed uneventfully for those still aboard with clear consciences, and then they put in at the much larger port of Corpus Christi before the day had gotten really hot. So all went ashore who might want to go ashore, the sea breezes blowing so much cooler than usual that morning and the skipper allowing they'd be there a good two hours.

Corpus Christi was a county seat, with a Ranger station and a number of pottery kilns, grain silos, and such. Mostly it was an old Mexican settlement, not incorporated as an Anglo town until '52. So lots of the older buildings as well as the Spanish churches were interesting to Anglo eyes, while the seaside Mexican market smelled tempting to any sort of nose with the weather suddenly so nice. So most of the off-duty crewmen as well as all the passengers but those same two honeymooners came on down the gangplank long before the furtive Hamp Godwynn made a sudden move ashore, moving like a rat down a ship's hawser—in the opinion of a lawman who'd apparently gotten off at Escondrijo.

Longarm hadn't. He'd had good old Norma Richards go ashore with his stuff to look after it and wire the Texas Rangers from that Coast Guard station at Escondrijo, while *he'd* gone on, holed up in her stateroom with the Saratoga trunk she'd entrusted to him. That big old trunk had been handy to hide his face under as he'd gone down the gangplank with it on his back.

So now Nora's trunk, like Longarm, stood behind a pile of lumber in the shade of a dockside loading shed as he waited for the killer in the Carlsbad hat to sidewind within hailing range with his own narrowed eyes darting about as if he wasn't dead certain he'd guessed right.

Longarm called out cheerfully, "You guessed wrong, Godwynn. So grab some sky if you'd like to be taken alive."

Godwynn spun on one boot heel and ran back toward the gangplank, zigzagging back and forth in case Longarm had really meant that.

Longarm had. He'd liked that pretty blonde. So he fired as the son of a bitch zagged, hoping to bust his ass and leave him in shape to explain why they'd wanted to gun a federal lawman.

He hit his intended target about where he'd intended, smack in the right cheek of his frantic ass. The heavy .44-40 slug spun the running killer like a mighty clumsy ballerina who'd come down wrong from her twirling, but Godwynn managed to get his right-hand gun out as he landed flat on his back, rolled, and staggered back to his feet, only to yelp like a kicked pup as he tried to put some weight down under his gun hand.

As he fired blind, chipping splinters off the far end of Longarm's lumber pile, the tall deputy called out, "Give it up, you poor simp! I don't want you dead. But I don't want you making it back to your rat hole aboard that steamer either. So drop that dumb gun and—"

Godwynn fired more certainly at the sound of Longarm's voice. So Longarm fired again, aiming at the wounded man's other leg this time.

He saw he'd hit the leg, if not the bone, when Godwynn let go of his Schofield to grab for his thigh with both hands and stagger for that gangplank some more bawling like a baby.

As Longarm broke cover, all too aware Godwynn still had a gun in his left holster, a distant voice called out, "Halt and explain all this in the name of the Texas Rangers!"

Longarm kept covering Godwynn as he strode out into the open after him, shouting back, "I'm the law too, trying to arrest me a mighty unreasonable cuss on murder in the first!"

So the white-shirted Ranger appearing down by the far end of that loading shed yelled, "Hot damn, we got us a *wire* on *that* one!" Then he fired his own Peacemaker, and being well trained as a marksman, if not as a careful investigator, hit Godwynn high in the chest with his longer but heavier shot. It likely would have left the wounded killer in piss-poor shape to talk had it been a lighter slug than 230 grains of lead backed by fifty-odd grains of powder, the Rangers tending to load their own shells and admiring noise at least as much as the Mexican *rurales*.

"I wish you hadn't done that," Longarm grumbled as they both met up near the cadaver sprawled on the dock at their feet.

The younger Ranger shrugged and said, "We both heard you warn him to give it up. Like I said, the famous federal marshal they call Longarm wired an all-points want on this one from just down the coast. Seems he murdered some passenger aboard that very steamer ahint you!"

Longarm said, "I know. I was there. I'm the one they call Longarm, and it was a government health worker I sent ashore in my place back at our last port of call. As she'd have wired you, this tricky son of a bitch could have swum ashore. But I figured he was hiding out somewhere on board. So I hid out just as good, and as you now see, he made a break for it here thinking I'd got off there."

The young Ranger made a wry face. "He must not have never hunted mice. Me and our old cat, when I was little, used to do what you just did. I'd stomp away whilst the smart old cat crouched silent by the mouse hole. Who was this mouse and how come he shot a lady aboard yonder steamer?"

Longarm hunkered down to go through the dead killer's pockets as he growled, "I suspicion he and his partner were out to get me and got her by mistake, God damn all three of us. I'm still working on it and . . . Damn it, his dead pard we put ashore at Escondrijo wasn't packing any infernal identification either!"

By this time lots of folks who'd ducked for cover at the sounds of gunplay were edging back out into the morning light. So Longarm added, "Stay here and make sure nobody steals the corpse whilst I go back aboard for their two stock saddles and possibles. All we can do now is put out as total a description of them and their gear as possible and hope for some answers."

The Ranger responded cheerfully, "Go ahead. Any number of my own pards ought to be here any minute, thanks to all that shooting. Ah, you'll tell the boys it was my bullet as finished the bastard, won't you?"

Longarm snorted, "You tell 'em. I was trying to take him alive. So he's all your own to keep and cherish. I got another boat to catch!"

Chapter 5

It wasn't that easy. He spent a good three hours making depositions for the local authorities, and then, once he was free to go to the Corpus Christi office of that same steam line, a prune-faced cuss in a wilted suit said he'd have to wire their main office in Galveston about his unusual request. When Longarm observed he hadn't needed special permission to just get aboard one of their coastal steamers down in Brownsville, the Corpus Christi booking agent explained, with a frosty smile, how the southbound steamer they expected around midnight was already overloaded with every stateroom spoken for.

Longarm said, "That's no problem, pard. I only got me and one old Saratoga trunk to get a hop, skip, and a jump down the coast. I don't mind standing up at the bar or, hell, the rail, till we get to Escondrijo. It was only a few hours coming up from there, and I was dying for a cool beer in that stuffy stateroom I'd holed up in."

The booking agent pursed his purple lips. "I'll have to clear it with the company. We're expecting heavy weather tonight and you wouldn't want to be by any rail in a full gale aboard a flat-bottomed coaster. They say those Chesapeake side-paddle steamers roll even worse in heavy weather, but I'll be damned if I can see how. So why don't you come back in a couple of hours and we ought to know by then if they'll have room for you."

Longarm frowned, "Well, I got some wires of my own I was

saving till I got to Escondrijo and mayhaps some answers about a dead man they're holding on ice down yonder as well. But I'm missing something about coastal traffic. The boat I come north aboard was almost empty. Yet you say this night boat you're expecting will be filled to overloading?"

The older man nodded patiently, "That northbound was just starting out. The southbound will have gone most of the way to its last stop at Brownsville."

Longarm shook his head. "Texas produces food and fiber in bulk, and consumes manufactured goods from the east in far more modest amounts in far more compact form. So how many piano rolls or even pianos would it take to fill the shelter deck and cold-storage hold of a southbound coaster that should have *delivered* most of its passengers and cargo by the time it neared the end of its run?"

The prune-faced cuss shrugged. "I only go by what they wire me from Galveston. Maybe a lot of people are headed for the mouth of the Rio Grande with a lot of stuff. I hear things are picking up down that way, what with the end of Reconstruction and the price of beef going through the roof. They've been putting in orange groves along our side of the river as well. Seems oranges grow swell in a hot sunny clime as long as they get plenty of irrigation water for their thirsty roots."

Longarm didn't want to talk about growing oranges, or even cows, along the lower Rio Grande. So he muttered he'd be back before sundown, and headed for the Western Union across the plaza.

He wired Billy Vail a fuller report than Norma Richards would have sent from Escondrijo. Then he wired Norma, care of the Western Union office down her way, that he'd be back with her trunk in time for her to catch the next northbound, Lord willing and they were wrong about that coming storm.

He got over to the noisy but shaded and colorful Mexican market in time for a noonday snack, and ate on the fly as he strolled from one good smell to the other, buying dribs and drabs of this and that, which he polished off, sitting down

46

at a small blue table in front of a cantina, with a tall cool schooner of *cerveza*. Mexican beer was the only thing that soft a man dared drink down there, unless it came to the table piping hot. The tamales, tapas, and such he'd picked up along the way had naturally been well cooked as well as fumigated with a ferocious amount of chili pepper.

As he sat there, enjoying the novelty of doing nothing about a damned thing for a spell, he became aware of two slightly ominous things at once. More than one passing Mexican called out casual warnings to secure the overhead awnings before *el huracán* arrived. And some Mexican kids kept peering around a taco stand at him as if he had two heads. He could only hope they found an Anglo sipping *cerveza* before a Mexican cantina an interesting novelty.

It was dumb for an Anglo with no fish to fry to hang around a Mexican neighborhood where he was getting stared at. So he finished his schooner sooner than he'd meant to, and got up to get going before anyone got up the nerve to act silly.

He thought someone already had when a ragged-ass boy in his teens with empty hands and an uncertain smile popped into view in front of him.

Longarm smiled back more coldly and growled, "*No me jodas, muchacho.* I don't want to marry your sister and these fucking boots are mine!"

The kid gulped and said, "I mean you no disrespect, *señor. Pero* you fit the description of an Anglo we were told to watch for here in Corpus Christi. We were wondering if by any chance you could be he."

Longarm moved casually to place his broader back against a 'dobe wall, and noticed nobody seemed out to edge around behind him as he replied, "*Quien sabe?* Everybody looks like somebody. Exactly who did you have in mind?"

The young Mexican said softly, "An Anglo lawman, a Deputy Long, known to our people as El Brazo Largo. He is said to despise El Presidente Diaz down in our old country as much as we do, despite his riding for Tio Sam. So La Bruja wishes him to know he is in danger he may know nothing about, and if you wish for to speak with her—"

"I'd rather you tell me here and now," Longarm cut in not too gently. "El Presidente Diaz is neither the first nor the last of your breed who ever tried to knife me in an alley, no offense. So I'll just pass on following you into any *barrio* for a powwow with a lady even *you* describe as what my folks call a *witch*."

The kid insisted, "La Bruja never comes out in the daytime. She seldom leaves her own *residencia* after dark. I do not know what it is La Bruja wishes for to warn you about. As you see, I am only her *mozo de mandados*. *Pero* she seemed most anxious for to have a word with you, and if you will not come with me I can only tell her I tried."

Longarm hesitated, then decided. "I ought to have my head examined for insufferable curiosity. But seeing it's broad daylight and you seem smart enough to know I'll take you with me no matter what your pals might hit me with . . . How far is this old witch of yours?"

The kid said the mysterious La Bruja lived on the far side of an old Catholic church across the plaza. So Longarm told the *mozo* to make sure his young pals didn't tag along too close, and repeated his warning with a thoughtful pat of his no-nonsense .44-40 as he let the kid lead the way.

As they crossed that plaza he got dust in his eye. The wind was really picking up now. It was the wrong time of the year for a hurricane down this way, if there was a right time to have a hurricane anywhere. But they did have summer storms along this coast that could qualify as mighty serious. So he hoped he wasn't fixing to get stranded here in Corpus Christi with good old Norma's trunk.

They circled the church, cut across a graveyard with some of the family tombs big enough to raise chickens in, and wound up in a maze of narrow walled-in *calles* just crooked enough to make you wonder. Both the older and newer parts of Corpus Christi lay on flat enough coastal plain. But the old Spanish-speaking builders had been free thinkers, tossing up one *casa* wrapped around a *pateo* here and another there, then filling in the lopsided spaces between with smaller and cheaper tenement courts. It was tougher to tell, in such *barrios*, how high on the hog folks might live. For rich or poor, none of the property owners to either side sprang for proper sidewalks, and one flat stucco wall topped with broken glass set in the mortar looked much the same as any other, no matter what lay on the other side.

His young guide led him not through one of the more imposing oak- or cypress-wood street entrances, but into a slot between what looked like two separate properties. At the far end of the gloomy passageway a smaller but stout-looking door had been deep-set in thick masonry. The kid knocked and the door swung inward, as if they'd been expected. But there was nobody visible in the dimly lit vestibule or on the flight of stairs winding down and lit by one wall sconce. It wasn't too clear which of four possible fort-like properties one was under as the stairs gave way to a long candle-lit corridor that seemed to have been laid out by a drunk trying to build straight.

As they neared a darker archway someone lit a candle on the far side of the beaded curtain across it, as if they'd been waiting up until then in the dark. Longarm smiled thinly at the theatrics of La Bruja. He wondered what the priests at that church near the plaza thought of the spooky way their neighborhood witch carried on. He knew they'd given up, down Mexico way, on trying to wean their simple folk of reliance on an odd mishmash of Roman and Aztec cures for what ailed them. He had more personal respect for the Mexican medicine men who described themselves as *curados*, who dosed sick folks with weeds and prayed to Christian saints and more pleasant Indian spirits. The ones claiming *brujeria* or powers of black magic did more harm than good with their love potions and such. But since this old witch said she wanted to help a friend of La Revolución, the least a man could do would be to listen politely. So he pasted a respectful smile across his face as he followed the kid through the beaded archway, to get smacked in the face with a disturbingly pleasant surprise.

La Bruja, if that was who he was smiling down on as she

reclined on a chaise in an outfit of black Spanish lace over velvet, was a breathtaking brunette of indeterminate age and likely pure Spanish ancestry. Her skin was even paler than that ivory shade high-toned Spanish ladies strove for, to show off darker aristocratic blood in their veins. She didn't look sick, but poor young Lenore Colbert hadn't looked that pale the other night slaughtered and drained.

The beautiful but mighty spooky lady waved Longarm to a hassock on his side of a low-slung coffee table, and said coffee and cakes were on their way. As he removed his hat and took his seat Longarm reconsidered calling her a lady. For the hassock was doubtless low-slung on purpose, to make the average guest look up to La Bruja as she held court atop that higher chaise. Longarm was a lot taller than average, and she still managed to sort of look down on him even while she was half reclining on one shapely side.

But Longarm had been sent to see the C.O. a lot in his army days, and he knew the way you got back at them for playing such games was to pay no mind.

So he just sat there, a politely questioning smile on his face, until La Bruja said, "Perhaps I should get right to the point in your own Yanqui manner, El Brazo Largo. I understand we are both on *simpatico* terms with such leaders of La Revolución as La Mariposa and El Gato?"

He shrugged. "Nobody with a lick of sense admires the current Administration of Old Mexico, *señorita*."

She sighed and said, "*Señora, por favor.* I am proud of the things my late husband did for the cause of Libre Mexico before *los rurales* shot him down like a dog against a wall. He and his brave comrades all refused the blindfold and faced their executioners with all of the scorn they deserved!"

Longarm nodded soberly. "I'm sure your average *rurale* firing squad deserves all the scorn they can get, *señora*. But didn't you say something before about getting to the point of this visit?"

She didn't answer as a much darker maid with more Indian features came in with a real silver salver piled with almond

50

cakes and a fine old silver service. There was some sort of family crest on the coffee urn. Longarm didn't try too hard to make it out. He didn't know too much about such notions to begin with, and family plate had a way of turning up far from its original family down Mexico way.

La Bruja dismissed her *chica* with a not unpleasant nod, and swung her satin slippers to the rug to sit properly as she poured a cup for Longarm. When he asked where her cup might be, she softly replied she didn't really care for coffee.

He could see she didn't mean to share the almond cakes with him either. So Longarm left both his coffee and cake untasted as well, murmuring something about just coming from the market and repeating his polite request they get to the point.

La Bruja said flatly, "An Anglo business associate of mine wants you dead. He offered me five hundred Yanqui dollars to have my own *muchachos* kill you. When I politely declined he raised the offer to a thousand."

Longarm whistled softly. "He must really want me dead. I've arrested many a gunslick who'd kill a man for less'n a hundred!"

La Bruja lay back on her chaise as if weary of the whole thing as she replied, "Not El Brazo Largo. I understand you got one of them on that steamer last night and killed the other one here in Corpus Christi this morning."

Longarm shook his head. "A frisky pup of a Ranger put the last fatal round in him. I was out to take him alive. I had an educated hunch they had to be working for somebody higher up, and I'd be much obliged if you'd tell me who that might be, seeing you surely know, *señora*."

La Bruja smiled reproachfully and sighed. "It was very cruel of God to leave us so far from Him and so close to *el gringo*. As I was just saying to that other one, your people and mine do not speak the same language even when they are speaking the same language. He was under the impression I was a mere criminal because I am required to bend just a few of your Yanqui laws in my efforts to fund political struggles in my own country. When I told him he would have to employ some other means,

51

we parted on mutually agreeable terms. It would be foolish for wolves to fight in a world of sheep, and he knew none of us would betray his identity to anyone. I don't think he expected me to warn you like this, of course. But please do not ask me to tell you any more about him."

Longarm nodded soberly. "I'm commencing to follow your drift. You don't aim to have either the local Anglo underworld or my old pal El Gato sore at you. So I'll just thank you for the warning and see what I can work out on my own."

But as he leaned his weight forward to rise, La Bruja sat up some more and insisted, "You can't be seen on the streets of Corpus Christi in broad daylight! It's true, as your enemies say, you may be on the alert for typical Anglo riders. But an enemy clever enough to think a *chico mejicano* might have better luck ought to be able to hire other types you might not take for assassins until too late!"

"The gang's mostly dressed sort of cow, eh?" Longarm mused as he perched undecided on the edge of that low hassock.

To which La Bruja replied with a knowing laugh, "Do not try to get it out of me with a, how you say, process of elimination. I have been questioned by serious policemen and have the scars to prove it. Nobody gets anything out of me that I do wish them to know."

Longarm nodded soberly. "I was sort of wondering about the dim lighting in here, *señora*. I said I understood the bind you were in. I ain't going to try and beat the identity of that murderous *pendejo* out of a lady who's offered me food, shelter, and such pleasant company. But I got my own fish to fry, and whether we savvy the same old lingo or not, another lady they shot the other night in my place was pretty as well as innocent. She'd never done them a lick of harm and it's my duty to see they're punished."

La Bruja insisted, "But the men who killed her in your stateroom *have* been punished! You shot them both yourself! The people they might have been working for never ordered them to kill anyone but you. Can't you see that?"

Longarm smiled thinly. "I see this mastermind told you more than I might have about our earlier transactions. If he wanted me dead before I gunned a couple of his boys, he must have thought I was already after him. So why can't we say who he might be?"

La Bruja laughed lightly, a sort of surprising sound, and archly replied, "You are as clever as they say you are. But it won't work. I will tell you frankly, it does not matter to me and mine whether you are on one Anglo's trail or another's. I only wish to see you leave Corpus Christi alive and well, should anyone south of the border ever ask. As I said, it is still broad daylight outside. You will stay here until dark. After sundown we can send you on your way to anywhere but the waterfront. They will be waiting for you along the docks, expecting you to try and board that midnight steamer."

He grimaced. "I got to board it. It's the only way I can get back down the coast to Escondrijo with a big Saratoga trunk!"

She smiled. "We can lend you a wagon and give you a map you would not be able to buy in any shop. People who deal in stolen goods along these shores do not wish to go through tedious customs declarations. So certain land routes that may appear more devious are somewhat safer. To begin with, nobody who does not know which route a traveler is taking would be in any position to ambush him, no?"

Longarm shrugged. "Your offer would be more tempting if it was only my own hide I was worried about, *señora*. But I'm the law and I'm paid to worry more about lawbreakers. Since I choose to doubt you and your own gang have busted any laws more serious than those of Texas and Old Mexico, we'll say no more about it. But murder on the high seas, or even a federal waterway, can't be constitutional to begin with, and they were trying to interfere with a federal agent on a government mission in any case."

He frowned thoughtfully and added, "Now, that's sort of odd as soon as you study on it. Why in thunder would they be so anxious to interfere in such a mundane mission? They surely

53

must have thought I was up to something else. That's happened before. There ain't nothing like a guilty conscience to make some crooks act guilty when it might have been smarter to just let a dumb lawman go on about his own dumb chores!"

La Bruja asked just what his mission might have been, if it hadn't been catching her so-called business associate.

He started to tell her, feeling no call to lie about a simple pickup of a prisoner. But as soon as he'd studied on it, he had to laugh. "Now who's pumping whom for secrets with innocent questions, no offense? It's been grand talking you in the dark, *señora*. But now I'd best go see if I can shed some daylight on all this skullduggery along the Fever Coast."

She rose with him, pleading, "Please don't go! There are too many of them out there for you or even your Ranger friends to handle! None of you know what you are up against and, look, if this is all some sort of mistake, as you suspect, you ought to be able to carry out your real mission in Escondrijo and be safely on your way home before they know where you've gone!"

He picked up his hat and put it on as she moved to block his way out with her petite pale form. "Stay! Just until sundown! Is there nothing I can do or say to keep you safe down here with me?"

He had to grin as he recalled a mighty similar scene from a swell spooky book he'd read a spell back. He said, "I don't reckon you really mean to offer me a chance at eternal life in odd company, if *life* is what they call Miss Carmilla's disturbing ways."

"Carmilla?" the pallid brunette demanded with a hurt look. "Are you comparing me to that . . . creature in that horror story by that French writer named Le Fanu?"

Longarm shook his head. "Irish, ma'am. I know it's an odd name for an Irishman, but that's what Sheridan Le Fanu is. He's written a heap of swell spooky yarns, and his story about Carmilla, written in '72 or so, is only one of 'em. His story about Uncle Silas is *really* creepy. You say you've read the one about Miss Carmilla?"

La Bruja suddenly looked even smaller as she sighed. "In a Spanish translation. A vicious woman in one of those endearing attempts to be humorous gave me her copy, asking if it reminded me of anyone we knew. I am called La Bruja by more simple people because I seem to have powers they do not understand. I avoid the sunlight because there is a price on my head and because I suffer a condition that runs in some noble Spanish families. Sunlight hurts my eyes and makes my skin break out in a frightening rash. I assure you I do not enjoy the taste of blood."

She hadn't said she didn't know what it tasted like, and Carmilla had told that young English gal in the book she only wanted to suck out her blood because she really liked her.

He'd read other books, there being little else to do a week or so before payday and the Denver Public Library being so well stocked. So he nodded soberly and said, "I've read about that inherited condition. I reckon it runs in noble families because rich folks don't have to go out and work by broad day whether they can stand it or not. I can see how more fortunate families, nursing their delicate skins indoors all day, and only coming out after dark to attend society doings in maybe a coach with heavy window drapes, might give rise to sillier stories about mysterious society ladies such as Miss Carmilla. But I know you ain't that sort of gal, so . . ."

"I'm not a lesbian vampire who turns into a black panther at will or sleeps all day in her coffin! I'm not! I'm not! I'm only a poor widow with a delicate skin condition!"

He tried not to laugh. It would have been rude to point out she had a whole gang of Mex border bandits as well. But his eyes must've twinkled, and she must've read his amused, mocking expression wrong. For she was suddenly stepping out of the satin and lace around her trim ankles, in no more than her long black socks and slippers as she grabbed him by both shirtsleeves and stared up wildly demanding, "Do you really take me for some blood-sucking lesbian, El Brazo Largo?"

He hauled her in and kissed her good, as most men would have, before he recalled how someone in that book had been about to do just the same to Miss Carmilla when he noticed the graveyard mold on her breath. La Bruja's soft parted lips smelled more like the almond cakes she'd doubtless had enough of before he'd arrived. It didn't hurt a bit to have her tonguing him so teasingly. So he tongued her back, and cupped a bare buttock in each big palm to hug her tighter to his jeans as she rubbed her small proud cupcakes over the front of his thin shirt. But once they'd come up for air he felt obliged to ask about that *chica* coming back for the coffee service neither one of them had bothered with.

La Bruja purred reassuringly that nobody ever pestered her and her guest unless she wanted them to, and asked him to follow her lead from such faint light as there was by her coffee table.

He was able to make out her pale hourglass form, floating ghostly above the frilly lace garters of her black thigh-length socks of jet-black lisle. Then she led the way to what looked more like a bed than that coffin Miss Carmilla had favored, and the next thing they knew he was driving something kinder than a wooden stake into her, further down, and she wasn't acting like Miss Carmilla at all.

The spooky lady in that story had spit blood and carried on just awful as she was getting penetrated in her coffin. But La Bruja kissed mighty sweet and moved her hips just right as he got her to come a good dozen hammerings ahead of him.

Once they both came, she agreed it would be even nicer if they both stripped down completely and started over with a black silk pillow under her ghostly but mighty warm little rump. So he didn't get to ask her about those Anglo crooks until he'd made them both come some more.

She still refused to tell him as they shared a cheroot with her disheveled head on his shoulder and free hand on his semi-erection. As she gently stroked his manly organ-grinder she pleaded, "Please don't try to take advantage of my weak nature, El Brazo Largo. I am already so ashamed of giving in to my own curious nature."

He hugged her bare flesh closer with the smoke gripped in

bared teeth as he said, "I'm still curious about them rascals out to kill me. What were you so curious about, *señora*?"

She giggled and confided, "You, *señor*. They say La Mariposa still brags insufferably about the many times she made El Brazo Largo come in her, down in Ciudad Mejico when they were hiding from *los rurales* in a railroad signal tower. Is that story true by the way?"

Longarm chuckled fondly and declared, "Truer than tales of a blood-sucking lesbian who can turn into a black panther on occasion, I reckon. It ain't polite to talk about screwing ladies who ain't here to defend themselves, and I never thought you were a lesbian to begin with."

She demurely asked if he was convinced she didn't like to suck, and when he allowed he was, she proved him wrong by sliding her head down his naked belly, long hair trailing, and proceeding to suck like all get out, although it wasn't his blood she was sucking.

So what with one pleasant surprise and another, Longarm wound up spending the rest of the day in the dark with La Bruja, and while he finally learned her real name and enough to lock her away for years, he never did get her to tell him who those other crooks were, or why they were after him, Lord love her.

Chapter 6

Longarm still would have done it his own way, weather permitting. But when he checked in at the steam line again that night, they told him none of their vessels would be coming or going till that heavy weather let up outside.

That sounded reasonable. The warm wet wind was blowing harder by the hour, and the heavy air smelled like spent brass cartridges, or a coming hurricane. So there was nobody laying in wait for him around the deserted wind-swept waterfront when he circled in silently from the lee side of some dark and shuttered warehouses with his gun out and his eyes slitted against the gathering storm.

When he got back to La Bruja's, she naturally wanted him to spend more time with her, and he was tempted. For he could likely come again if he really set his mind and lush lips to it. But he insisted on holding her to that other promise, and so it was along about quarter past midnight, with neither coastal steamers nor paid killers to be seen in the swirling darkness, when Longarm finally left by way of a clamshell-paved wagon trace to the south, driving a team of Spanish mules as he hunkered half sheltered by a flapping canvas wagon cover with old Norma's Saratoga trunk and some trail supplies in the wagon box behind his sprung seat.

He commenced having second thoughts about the grand notion a mile or less outside of town, when the light got even worse and he had to take the word of the mules and the gritty sounds of the steel-rimmed wheels that he was still following that shell path through what seemed like a mighty herd of wind-whipped palmettos flapping fronds on all sides as they strove to uproot their fool selves and take off like stampeding bats.

It got too dark to see even that much as the wind howled ever louder, and then the invisible mules out ahead balked at hauling him and old Norma's Saratoga another step, no matter how a man snapped the ribbons on their wet rumps and shouted curses into the gathering storm. So he set the brake, hitched the ribbons around its shaft, and got down to see what had gotten into the fool mules.

He said he was sorry for calling them foolish as soon as he could make out what they hadn't wanted to get into. The shell road ended in a wind-lashed sheet of muddy water, with no far side in sight. Nobody with a lick of sense would pave the way to the bottom of a river on purpose. So it was safe to assume the gale-force winds had run a high tide further ashore than usual. Winds did that some along the gulf coast. Wind surges along a low swampy shore made for more deaths than getting hit by flying shit in your average hurricane.

He led the mules back up the wagon trace afoot for a ways as he told them, "I'm wet too. So the question before the house is whether we head back to town and lose Lord knows how much time, or keep going in hopes there's another route and we stumble over it before all three of us drown?"

The mules offered no suggestions. Once he had them on as high a stretch of wagon trace as there seemed to be for miles, Longarm got back up under the flapping canvas to dig out that soggy map and some fortunately waterproof matches.

Longarm favored a brand of Mexican wax-stemmed matches because you just never knew when you'd need a light in damp weather, although weather as damp as *this* was a tad unusual. Mexicans made really fine candles too, and the first match he struck burned more like a tiny candle than your average match. But he still had to strike three in a row above the map spread atop Norma's Saratoga trunk before he was certain there was no other wagon trace around that normally fordable tidal creek.

He refolded the map and put it away, muttering, "Well, maybe La Bruja will serve us some hot chocolate. We sure as shit ain't going any farther south just yet!"

But as he swung his long legs over the sprung seat to brace one instep against the brake shafts while he unhitched the wet slippery ribbons, he saw a bright point of light through the flailing palmetto fronds to his west.

He called out. There was no way to tell if he'd been heard, or if anyone had answered amid all the flapping, moaning, and groaning all about. So he released the brake, but left the ribbons hitched as high and dry as he could manage as he got down some more to take the near mule by the cheek strap and declare, "That's a house or at least a camp about a quarter mile off, pard. Even if they can't set us on another trail, they might be able to shelter us from this storm and save us a few hours when and if it ever lets up."

He started leading the storm-lashed and balky team toward the distant light. It wasn't easy because even he could see they were off any sort of beaten path and sort of floundering through eight- or ten-foot palmettos, chest-high sea grape, and ass-high sacaguista—as they called this particular breed of salt grass.

The mules perked up and began to act more sensible as they too detected human life and possible shelter up ahead. Longarm recalled what that purser had told him about the sort of humans squatting out here on the coastal plain. Moreover, it was still considered dumb, as well as impolite, to drop in on strangers after dark without any advance notice. So lest they take him for raiding Comanche or worse, Longarm drew his .44-40 and fired three times at the overhead winds. Three shots was the accepted way one shouted for help or attention out this way. One or two shots figured to be a distant hunter who'd as soon not have company as he went about his own beeswax. But three in a row meant a piss-poor shot if it was a hunter. So folks tended to assume whatever was going on might be *their* own beeswax as well.

60

Longarm knew he was right when he heard a distant gun reply to his above the wind. As he forged on, awkwardly reloading with his chilled wet hands full of mule as well, he mused out loud, "Outlaws on the run would be more likely to douse their light and lay low than answer back. But that don't mean we're the pals they left that lamp in the window to welcome. So we'd best just tether you and Norma's Saratoga out here amid the swaying palmettos a ways. I just hate to chase after mules spooked by gunplay."

He led them another furlong, then paused by a stout clump of beach plum to tether his borrowed team a rifle shot out from what he now recognized as a pressure lamp burning inside the wet canvas cover of another wagon, this one a third bigger than the Studebaker La Bruja had lent him. So what in thunder might a fellow traveler need a full-blown freight wagon for way off the beaten path like this?

As he waded closer through the tall wet grass a chili-flavored voice called out, "*Quien es?* Is that you, Mathews?"

To which Longarm could only reply, "Not hardly. I answer to Custis Long and I've run out of better places to go in this storm."

There was no answer. Longarm moved closer anyway, and finally heard a cautious "*Habla usted español, extranjero mio?*"

Longarm spoke Spanish better than he wanted to let on to any Mexican who called him a stranger so sarcastically. So he called back, "If you're talking to me, speak American, boy. For I'm sorry to say this here is America, not Mexico, no offense."

There was another thoughtful silence as Longarm moved closer, a tad thoughtful himself. Then another voice called out, "We have been expecting for to meet another Anglo here. A short red-bearded hombre driving an ox-drawn *carreta*?"

Longarm answered easily as well as honestly, "Ain't seen nobody but my own fool self out in this damned storm since I left Corpus Christi against the advice of more sensible folk. The wagon trace I thought I was following to Escondrijo wound up underwater. Might you boys know another route by way of higher ground?"

His unseen challenger called back, "No. We are on what your kind calls the Southern Cattle Trail. It runs from Corpus Christo to El Paso and beyond, by way of San Antonio and Del Rio. It does not lead south to Escondrijo. If the regular trail to the south is flooded, we suggest you turn back. But tell us, are you alone out here, Tejano?"

Longarm allowed he was. He had no call to inform them he wasn't exactly a Texan. He didn't speak Spanish well enough to tell folks of one part of Mexico from those of another either.

Knowing how some Mexicans felt about some Texicans, he was taken aback when he was suddenly invited on in for coffee and grub before he headed back to town. But it would have been impolite to move in on such an invite with his six-gun out. So he left it holstered, and contented himself with his double derringer concealed in one big fist as he strode on over.

As he got close enough to make out three Mexicans lined up between him and their big covered wagon, he decided the young kid to his right would have to be the first target. The two older ones were more likely to act sensible once they saw he had the drop on them. But you just never knew what a kid was likely to do, as the late Joe Grant should have known when he tried to bully Billy the Kid that time in Fort Sumner. Kids just had no respect for their elders, and considered a rep like Joe Grant's a challenge.

All three were grinning at him like shit-eating dogs, and he saw no evidence of a chuck fire on the soggy soil beside their lamp-lit wagon. Then one called out, "Come on, Tejano. We'll give you plenty of coffee before we send you on your way!"

Longarm was glad he'd elected to play dumb when the other older one asked conversationally in Spanish, "Don't you think he's close enough now?"

The friendly-acting leader replied as casually, "Why put more holes than we need to in such a nice shirt?"

Then the kid smirked and purred, "I have a better idea. Why not take him alive, make him take all his clothes off, and have some fun with him first?"

By now Longarm was within easy pistol range, so he took a steady stand in the rain with the wind at his back as he raised the over-and-under muzzles of his derringer into their lamplight and announced in no-nonsense Spanish, "I have a better idea. All three of you are going to politely unbuckle your gunbelts, let your guns fall where they may, and step clear of them right now."

It was the kid, of course, who pointed out, "He's right about there being three of us, and I only see two barrels for that whore pistol!"

The sly talker of the bunch sighed and muttered, "Feel free to be the first one he shoots, Juanito! I assure you I'll get him after he gets you and Robles."

Longarm growled, "I told you what I wanted you to do. I am not going to tell you again. So do it or die, right now!"

None of them wanted to die. So once he'd disarmed them with his derringer, Longarm switched to his six-gun and reached for the handcuffs riding the back of his gun rig with his left hand, telling them in the English he was more comfortable with, "First things first, we'd best make sure nobody's led into more temptation."

He tossed the unlocked cuffs to the kid, who caught them without thinking as Longarm commanded, "I want you to snap one of those steel rings around the right hand of Robles there. What are you waiting for, a boot in the ass?"

The kid did as he was told. Once he had one of his elders cuffed, Longarm herded all three of them to a rear wheel of the big freight wagon and explained what came next. The still-uncuffed leader, whose name was something like Lamas, protested, "This is most cruel! Why not inside the wagon, or at least on the other side, out of the wind?"

Longarm smiled mirthlessly and replied, "What are you crying about? Has anyone offered to corn-hole you, or even steal your shirt? Both you bigger boys hunker down by that wheel, face to face on opposite sides of the spokes. Once Juanito cuffs your right wrists together, with the links through the spokes, even dumb bastards like you ought to see the reason in my madness."

They did, bitching like hell, well before the kid had them cuffed together, squatting on either side of the wheel in the wet wind-whipped grass. Once Longarm saw he'd secured them, he turned to the kid and pistol-whipped the mean little shit to the ground a few paces off. He kicked the downed punk in the ribs, saying, "You can get back up now. I won't smack you no more unless you offer me a whisper of your smart-ass sass!"

As Juanito got back to his feet, both hands to his busted lips, Longarm asked if he had anything sassy to say.

When Juanito sobbed he'd do anything Longarm wanted, including a few offers Longarm hadn't been considering, the tall deputy laughed and said, "I like gals better. Right now I want to go to Escondrijo, and seeing you boys know this swampy range so much better, here's what we're going to do."

Waving the dripping muzzle of his six-gun at the two wet rats hunkered in windswept misery at the rear of the heavy wagon, he explained. "You're going to guide me through this stormy night to where I want to go, Juanito. I'll kill you at the first suspicion we ain't headed the right way, and Lord only knows what'll ever happen to these pals of ours. Must get hot and thirsty as hell around here when the sun comes back in the Texas sky after a storm."

Hunkered by the wheel, Lamas bitched, "You can't do that to fellow *cristianos, señor*! Nobody but a Comanche would kill anyone as slow as that!"

Longarm said, "I ain't finished. So all three of you listen tight. When and if Juanito gets me safe and sound to Escondrijo, I mean to turn him loose with the key to them cuffs. If he knows the way down to Escondrijo he ought to know the way back. You'll wind up with a free set of handcuffs instead of my shirt and rosy red rectum. So I'd best take your guns and pocket money in exchange."

They protested it wasn't fair to rob them at gunpoint the way they'd been planning to rob *him*. He just laughed. When young Juanito asked if he might have his own pony to ride both ways, Longarm thought that was sort of funny too. He said, "It ain't too far for you to make on foot in one day, if you really put your mind to it."

When Juanito insisted it would take him at least eighteen hours, Longarm just shrugged and said, "We'd best be on our way then. For I suspicion these pals of yours will be hot and thirsty as all get out by the time you hoof it all the way back with the key to them cuffs."

Chapter 7

The storm let up before sunrise. It still took longer to make it to Escondrijo by way of Juanito's longer route through higher range to the west. By then they'd spent enough time together, with nothing better to do than talk, for Longarm to have gotten a handle on what Juanito and the others had been doing out in all that rain.

They were gun runners, waiting for a load of British Enfield rifles they meant to smuggle across the border up above Laredo. Longarm had a notion he knew the unguarded stretch they'd had in mind. He knew a Mexican rebel depending on the *federale* troops he fought for ammunition favored the same brand of rifles most *federales* still used. Mexico had gotten a swell buy on Enfields, considering what they cost folks who meant to for pay for them sooner or later. Old Sam Colt had known enough to demand cash on the barrel head for the horse pistols *los rurales* got to fire at pigs and chickens on their way through many a sullen village.

Finally Longarm spied church spires and chimney smoke against the sunrise to their east. He turned to Juanito and said, "That Scotch poet was right about the best-laid plans of mice and men, you mean little shit. I was fixing to wire the Rangers and have 'em waiting for you by the time you hiked all the way back."

"That is not the deal we made!" protested the unhappy youth.

But Longarm replied, "Yes, it was, as soon as you study the small print. I'm a lawman and the three of you confessed right out, albeit in Spanish, you were fixing to waylay me and worse. But I ain't finished. I may be a lawman, but I suffer from this rough sense of justice, and there ain't no justice down Mexico way with that piss-faced Porfirio Diaz calling his fool self El Presidente, as if he'd been elected, the lying son of a bitch."

Juanito turned on the seat they were sharing. "You know this much about my poor country and her poor people, *señor*?"

Longarm shrugged and replied, "Not as well as I might if I'd been born that unfortunate, I'll allow, but well enough to suspicion most any government you rebels could come up with would have to be some improvement. So getting back to the deal we made, I reckon I'm going to have to keep it the way you thought I meant it, with no small print. You can save yourself better than an hour afoot if you get off right here and get going whilst it's still cool. Grab one of them canteens in the back, and what the hell, you ought to be able to pack along a few tortillas. A lady I know rolled some in wax paper for me back in Corpus Christi. So here's the damn key, grab what you need and just *git*! What are you waiting for, a good-bye kiss?"

The kid rummaged in the wagon box for the water and trail grub as he murmured, "I do not understand you at all, *señor*. I mean, now that I recall our earlier conversation, I see what you mean by small print. Is true you only said you would turn me loose with this key. You never said you would not tell the Rangers we were *ladrónes*, or where we might be found. *Pero* what has changed your mind about us?"

To which Longarm could only reply, "I haven't changed my mind about you. I still think you're three *mierditas* who'd be a disgrace to your families if anyone could say who your fathers might have been. But you ain't the only Mex rebels I've ever met, and some of the ones I like better may need them rifles before El Presidente steps down of his own free will. So *adios*, shithead, and shoot a *federale* for me, if you have the balls."

Juanito dropped off the far side with Longarm's generous issue of water and trail grub and the handcuff key in a pocket.

Then he said, "I think I know who you must be now. My people speak of a *muy gringo* but *simpatico* Yanqui they call El Brazo Largo."

Longarm didn't answer. He just snapped the ribbons to drive on to town, leaving Juanito to stand there, making the sign of the cross, as he marveled, "*Jesus, Maria y Jose!* I threatened to screw El Brazo Largo before I killed him and I am still alive! They are right about him. The man is a goddamn saint!"

Longarm didn't hear that, which was just as well. For he already felt sort of guilty about it being such a beautiful morning. All that wind from the sea had left the coastal plain smelling cool and clean as a whistle, with the salt grass dewy and lightly grazed this far out of town. He spied a few widely scattered sea lions, as longhorns grazing the swampy coast ranges were called by Texicans. Some of them stared back at him wall-eyed, but none of them shied off at the sight of a mule-drawn wagon.

Longarm felt a moment of concern for the Mexican kid he'd just dropped off afoot this close to any kind of free-ranging beef critters. For your average longhorn was as likely to charge a man afoot as it was to flee anyone on a cow pony. But while a dude could get in a heap of trouble around cows, mounted as well as afoot, most Mexicans found dancing the fandango with beef on the run an interesting challenge. Most of them were good at it. It didn't take a college degree to tell when a beef critter was fixing to charge with murderous intent. They never really meant it unless their four hooves came together under their centers of balance as their tails went up and their heads went down so they could sort of fall towards you with most of their weight before they commenced to play Express Train. So once you were sure they were coming at you, hell bent and head down, the idea was to get the hell off the tracks.

He spied more cows grazing on shorter salt grass as he rolled closer to the rooftops of the awakening town with the sun in his eyes. He knew that steamer he'd come north on had just picked up a load of freshly slaughtered beef in Escondrijo. So that was likely why they were spread so thin on heavily grazed range. The sea lions that had been spared looked a tad lean but healthy enough. So they'd likely been passed over for now to fatten up a mite before they wound up refrigerated.

"Enjoy life whilst you can, cows," he called out aloud, although not without any sympathy at all. It was hard not to feel just a tad sorry for any critter whose only purpose in life was to be slaughtered and butchered for human consumption. But as soon as you studied on it, you could see there'd have never been a tenth as many domestic brutes, from cows to chickens, if humankind had never learned how swell they tasted.

Some cows tasted more tender than Texas longhorns, although few other breeds enjoyed the taste of Texas grass. It took a tough cow to thrive on such tough range, although both the grass and beef grew just a tad more tender within the salty smell of the Texas shores. The long-horned sea lions all about might have had a better hold on the beef market if it hadn't been for the fevers that seemed to go with such green and muggy grazing.

The Fever Coast seemed to be the breeding grounds for more than one mean ague. One of the meanest was a spleen-rotting cow plague known as Spanish fever in Texas and Texas fever everywhere else.

Longhorns in general and the coastal sea lions in particular seemed immune to Texas fever, which made them about as welcome as a lit cigar in a hayloft in other parts, where folks were trying to raise shorthorn or dairy breeds that just curled up and died when they caught it.

Whether they cottoned to Kansas views on Texas fever or not, the ranchers raising Texas beef along this Fever Coast were maybe twice as firm about the hoof-and-mouth plague carried by healthy-looking cows out of Old Mexico. Nobody was sure about the causes of either. But as in the case of Texas fever, hoof-and-mouth seemed to hide out in immune stock between disastrous outbreaks that could slaughter whole herds and make them unfit to even skin for hides. Stock known to have either highly contagious disease had to be shot and buried deep. That was the law, state or federal. Nobody with a lick of sense wanted to risk the whole Western cattle industry with the price of beef rising ever higher back in the booming East.

By the time he was within three miles, or an easy hour's walk on foot, of those rooftops along the lagoon, he saw more corn, beans, and peppers growing all around than cows. Most such *milpas* or small truck fields in these parts were tilled by Mexican hoe farmers. That seemed the way most Mexican folks liked to farm, living in close-knit villages or their own *barios* of larger towns so they could walk out to their scattered *milpas*. He wasn't sure whether Mexicans stuck to such habits because they were backward or because it made a certain sort of sense. The Anglo Homestead Act had never been tried in Old Mexico, and a Mexican played hell trying to file a homestead claim with the U.S. Bureau of Land Management unless he brushed up on his English or, failing that, convinced some land office clerk he was a dumb Dutchman or Swede. So that was a likely reason you seldom saw isolated Mexican farmhouses off on some lonely quarter section. And there was something to be said for having one's cash crops scattered among, say, half a dozen smaller holdings. For even as he passed some corn *milpas* flattened by the recent storm, he spied others where, from some natural whim, the green young cornstalks still stood proud in the morning sun. Mexican hoe farmers were independent thinkers when it came to what they had growing in a particular plot too. So unlike many a homesteader with all his seed money tied up in one cash crop, his more casual Mexican competitor, growing all sorts of stuff in modest amounts, could neither make a killing on a rising market in, say, popcorn or get wiped out in, say, a corn-borer plague.

He passed a cactus-fenced field where a small ragged-ass kid was overseeing a half-dozen young hogs, likely from the same litter, as they rooted in a wind-flattened and rain-flooded bean field for such value as that storm had left. A few fence lines along he saw some goats, tethered on long lines, already starting to tidy up a ruined corn *milpa* by consuming the still-green stalks so they could wind up as goat cheese or gamy meat. Mexicans liked both more than your average Anglo did, but nobody could eat smashed and sun-dried cornstalks unless he or she was a goat.

Longarm didn't see any serious stock, or serious stockmen, on the modest Mexican *milpas* this close to Escondrijo. But he didn't find that odd. You had to get out of Denver a ways, maybe a half a day by produce wagon, before you came to more spread-out cattle spreads.

He didn't know whether such outfits in these parts would turn out to be Mexican or not. He knew anyone owning a big enough beef operation to matter would have to be Anglo-Texican, for the same reasons it was risky to one's health to spread out across much range in Old Mexico unless one was an Old Mexican. But while one seldom saw Anglo buckaroos riding for Mexican outfits to the south, a lot of big Texas outfits hired Mexican *vaqueros*, who worked cheaper as well as better than many an Anglo top hand.

Thinking about that led Longarm into thinking about various Texas cow towns of a surly nature on your average Saturday night. But Billy Vail hadn't sent him all this way to see how the local Mexican and Anglo cowhands got along. He just had to see whether Deputy Gilbert and their prisoner, wanted in Colorado, were fit to get on back there.

He'd have to track down old Norma Richards and give her this old Saratoga, of course, and maybe by now the Rangers had some notion as to why some asshole up in Corpus Christi had such a hard-on for an out-of-state lawman only trying to do his job.

He hoped they had. He was cursed with a curious nature, and he knew Billy Vail would never abide him wasting enough time to matter if Rod Gilbert and Clay Baldwin were fit to travel.

The wagon trace rumbled him onto a simple plank bridge across a tidal creek half choked with tall spartina reeds. He could see some windows under the rooftops ahead now. He'd have doubtless felt a bit closer to town if it hadn't been for a swamping cactus hedge on the far side of the creek. Then a skinny young gal of the Mexican persuasion ran out onto the wagon trace, long black hair unkempt, white cotton frills all aflutter, and bare feet really moving, until she spied Longarm coming with that wagon and reversed direction toward him screaming for help, a lot of help, in a hurry.

Longarm let the mules haul him on to meet her as he called out to her, "*Que pasa? En que puedo servirle, señorita?*"

To which she replied in English no worse than his Spanish, "Is my father. He has been bitten by a beast and we cannot stop the bleeding!"

Longarm reined in long enough to extend a strong hand and haul the small but nubile young gal up beside him. She likely didn't notice, and so he never commented on the one tawny tit the two of them managed to expose getting her aboard. As she sat down beside him, Longarm already had the mules swinging through the opening in the cactus she'd just popped out of. But as he headed for the rambling row of brushwood *jacales* and corrals across eight or ten acres of beans and corn, his distraught guide pointed off to their west, telling him, "Me *padre* is over that way, closer to the water."

Longarm saw no water. But an older and fatter version of the gal beside him was huddled with two younger boys over something or somebody down in the knee-high peppers they had growing in that corner to his right. So he looked for a good way through their modest crops, and then, as the worried gal beside him said not to worry about the damned old beans, he drove right over.

One of the boys took the reins as Longarm followed the daughter of the house over the side. He was sort of sorry he had as soon as he caught sight of the stocky middle-aged Mexican sprawled there in the mud and crud with his white cotton pants and right leg torn all to hell.

Longarm saw they'd improvised a rope tourniquet around the stocky farmer's muscular upper thigh. He could only wonder how much worse the poor cuss could bleed with nothing at all wrapped above the ghastly wounds around his busted or dislocated knee. He told the English-speaking girl, "We have to get him to a doctor in town *muy pronto*. We ain't got a litter. We ain't got time to make one. So tell him this is going to hurt and ask your brother there to lower the tailgate of that wagon box."

She did, in a rapid singsong he'd have never managed on his own in a lingo he had to sort of feel his way along in. The badly injured Mexican bit his lower lip and hissed like a steam kettle, but never let on how bad it really must have felt as Longarm picked him up, with some effort, and shoved him gently as possible into the wagon behind the trunk. Then the young gal raised the tailgate and ran around to the front, calling out, "*Abordos y vamonos pa'l carajo!*"

So the old gal and all three kids scrambled aboard as best they could as Longarm drove back across their already battered crops.

The young gal wound up seated beside him some more as her mother in the back hung on to her injured man, sobbing at Longarm to go "*mas rapido!*" but also crying "*cuidado!*" as he did his best, without any advice, to follow the wheel ruts as fast as he safely could.

The young gal explained that the poor *mamacita* was upset, but that she knew how kind and thoughtful he was trying to be to people he'd never been introduced to.

He assured her he followed her *mamacita*'s drift, and added, "She has every right to be unsettled by that fearsome bite out of *papacito's* poor leg. What in thunder did he tangle with back there, a tushy old sow with a litter she was guarding amid them peppers?"

The girl shook her head. "I do not know what the beast is called in your tongue. We call *aligador!*"

Longarm whistled softly. "That's close enough to alligator if we're talking about the same critter. I'd heard they could be found all around the Gulf of Mexico from Florida to Yucatan but . . . out in the middle of a pepper crop?"

She sighed. "Is a *bahia pequeña*, what you call a tidal creek, I think, just beyond our back *seto* . . . you say hedgerow, no?"

When he said that sounded close enough, she explained, "*Las aligadoras* come out on land for to sun themselves when the weather is as cool as this morning. *Pero*, like yourself, Papacito

73

was surprised to find such a big one on our side of the cactus *seto* when he went out for to look at our poor peppers. It grabbed him before he knew it was there, and he thinks it was trying to take him home for to feed its own family. They were rolling all over when the rest of us rushed out for to see what Papacito was cursing about. My brother, Miguelito, beat *la aligador* many times with a hoe, a steel-bladed hoe, before it let go and slid back through the cactus into the *bahia*. Miguelito is only twelve, but *muy macho*, just like Papacito!"

Longarm smiled thinly and said, "They both must have been. I'd say that gator was unusually *macho* as well. They ain't supposed to act so bold as a rule. Has anyone you know been feeding 'em around here?"

"Feeding, *señor*? You have heard of people who would actually feed such dangerous beasts? One would have to be *loco en la cabeza*, no?"

He shrugged. "Greenhorns likely feel they're just out to be neighborly. But they got signs posted over Galveston way that warn folks not to do so, lest you get them gators really dangerous."

He could see a street intersection down at the far end of their hedged-in wagon trace now as he continued. "They say gators get to coming in when they get used to hearing splashes at a particular bridge, boat dock, or whatever. Makes it more dangerous than usual should a dog, or kid, fall in. The critters aren't inclined to consider before they snap, left to their own unkindly natures. Do I have to explain further why it's not so wise to feed 'em until they lose their natural caution?"

She shuddered and reminded him she and her kin had just pulled a family member out of a sassy gator's jaws.

He nodded. "That's my point. Their more usual diet would be fish, ducks, muskrats, and such. So the critter as just went for your dad must have picked up such bad habits around other humans. I don't know my way around Escondrijo. Which way do we swing when we get to that cross street ahead?"

She said the *curado* they usually went to dwelt down to the right.

He said, "No offense, *señorita*, but your old man don't need any herbs or even prayers right now. He needs surgical stitching, considerable surgical stitching, by a surgical sawbones trained gringo in manner, if not a pure gringo by birth!"

She sobbed, "I never called you a gringo, *señor. Pero*, since you are the one who brought it up, is no *cirujano gringo* in Escondrijo who would treat a greaser, as I think you call us."

He said, "I don't call colored folk niggers either. But I follow your drift. So which way might that Coast Guard station be from here?"

She didn't follow his drift before he'd repeated Guardia Costa in her own lingo. Then she said, "I thought that was what you meant. Is *a la izquirda, pero* very far, and even if we get there in time I do not think they will wish for to take Papacito in!"

Longarm swung the team left onto the cross street, which seemed the only important north-south thoroughfare in the dinky collection of sun-silvered frame buildings as he assured the injured man's oldest child, "I don't care if they want to take him in or not. I aim to tell them they have to. I'm a U.S. deputy marshal, here on federal business, and I reckon I can say who may or may not be a federal witness under federal protection and hence eligible for emergency medical treatment at any infernal federal clinic I can find!"

She told him he was talking too fast for her to follow his English. He wasn't up to explaining all that in Spanish. So he just drove on, faster than folks usually drove through town and hence attracting a lot of stares and a good deal of cussing as they tore on up the dirt-paved street.

Then, as they were passing what seemed a big whitewashed warehouse, Longarm spotted a familiar figure in white and reined in to call out to Norma Richards, "Hey, Doc? I got your Saratoga trunk and a man in dire need of medical attention here. Your move!"

The motherly but sort of handsome older gal stared thunderstruck for just a bit before she called back, "Custis, is that you, with my lab equipment at last, praise the Lord?"

As she dropped lightly down from the loading platform of that odd warehouse and moved toward them in her already muddy high-buttons, she declared, "I'd just about given you and my microscope up for lost. We're in a lot of trouble here, Custis. As you see, I've been able to commandeer this empty icehouse for use as an emergency ward but without proper lab equipment—"

Then Longarm was down off the wagon to steer the educated lab technician around to the tailgate as he tersely explained, "Don't take no microscope to see what's ailing this customer I brought you. But for the record, those teeth marks all over his right knee were left by a gator, not one of Doc Finlay's mosquitos!"

When Longarm unfastened the tailgate, the well-rounded Norma got up under the canvas with surprising grace and proceeded to rip what was left of Papacito's pants off below that tourniquet. As she took in the full extent of the Mexican's injuries she whistled softly, then declared, "They do tend to overdo things here in Texas. We have to get that tourniquet off if we're to save that leg. But first we have to tie off some arteries and make a hundred and fifty stitches, minimum. So we'd better get him inside, on the table, the day before yesterday!"

She added something about going inside for a pair of stretcher bearers. But Longarm was already following her with the chunky but smaller man in his arms, like an injured child. So Norma told all of them to follow and they did, like a worried line of ducklings.

It was warmer inside than out, despite the gloom under the bare wooden trusses holding up the big cork-lined roof. Longarm saw lots of the heat had to be rising from the hundred-odd folks filling most of the folding cots spread across the sawdust floor. Nobody had more than a sheet covering them. But some were twisting like worms caught on a tile walk by a baleful rising sun. The smell was disgusting as well. Pine oil and fresh linens could only do so much when folks took to puking and shitting all over themselves and a sawdust floor.

As Norma led the newcomers through some hanging sheets and into a corner she'd improvised as a sort of lab and autopsy or operating room, Longarm glanced up through the gloom and said, "You say this here is supposed to be an *icehouse*, Doc?"

Norma pointed at two kitchen tables with a door across them. "Make him as comfortable as you can there while I scrub up again. They tell me they used to store ice from New England here, before that meat packer down the other way installed ice-making machinery a year or so ago. I commandeered this layout as soon as they assured me it was the nearest we could get to a hospital ward here in town. That Coast Guard clinic is too small as well as too far away. This space is too small for all these repeat customers we keep getting, bless their fevered brows."

Longarm told the four Mexican folks they'd best wait outside. None of them argued. But as the older daughter ducked out Norma said, "Me and my direct approach. I didn't mean every one of them. Somebody who can speak both languages might save us a wrestling match here."

Longarm allowed he could likely translate any medical jargon a hoe farmer was likely to understand, so the motherly-looking Norma swung around from her washstand with a lethal-looking load of cutlery on an enameled tin tray, saying, "I'm low on morphine to begin with, and the dosage can be tricky when a patient's in shock after losing Lord knows how much blood. So I want you to tell him it would be better if I irrigated and sutured his wounds without any anesthetic. Tell him he won't feel much more pain than . . . well, a whole lot of pinpricks."

Longarm moved to the far side of the improvised operating table, nudged the semi-conscious Mexican, and told him they were going to have to hurt him. Since he was talking to a grown man, not a crybaby, he felt no call to bullshit about pinpricks.

The badly bitten farmer smiled gallantly up at the woman in white and croaked, *"Que bella es. Quando comienza?"*

Longarm said, "He thinks you're pretty and wants to know why you ain't started, Miss Norma."

So she picked up a wet sponge and wrung it out over the gory mess. The liquid rinsing blood and crud from the lacerations looked like water. Longarm suspected it was something stronger when the man on the table stared thunderstruck and shouted, *"Ay, mierda! Eso es una mierda!"*

So Longarm assured the old gent it was more likely alcohol than the shit he suspected. But he doubted the Mexican heard him. As he shot a questioning glance across the table, Norma Richards assured him, "Only comatose. Just as well. I want to suture these torn arteries before I unfasten that tourniquet, and that's the part that seems to inspire unpleasant remarks about a poor old woman who means well."

As he watched her clean, skilled fingers mend the ends of what a lay man could take for bloody macaroni, he said, "Aw, you ain't so old, considering how much training it would take to get so good with that curvy needle, Miss Norma. But no offense, whatever happened to the doctors, military and civilian, in these parts?"

She irrigated the unconscious man's knee some more as she made a wry face and said, "The pharmacist's mate in command of the Coast Guard clinic is just outside, running a fever we can't get down with quinine sulfate, if that's what's in those brown bottles he issued me before he was stricken himself. Now that you've brought my own medical supplies, however limited, I may be able to get a handle on what on earth they've all been coming down with!"

He said he'd be glad to get his own possibles back, and asked what had happened to the civilian docs a town this size would surely have.

She picked up a smaller needle and began to close the wounds of the ripped-open farmer as she said simply, "There were three, they say. I never met any of them. One died and the other two skipped out before I got off that coastal steamer a million years ago. They say the local doctor who caught it and died had been the only one trying to fight whatever it is we're fighting. The other two said there was no use risking the lives of themselves and their families on something they just didn't understand."

She rinsed away more blood and made another skillful stitch as she pensively added, "Maybe they had a point. The oath all physicians take makes no mention of running off and leaving patients to die, but it happens. You should have seen the stampede we had over to the northeast in New Orleans in the last bad yellow fever outbreak."

Longarm nodded soberly. "I heard. This fever we got here in Escondrijo ain't like yellow jack?"

She shook her head, either unaware of or not caring about the one soft brown strand of hair on her sweat-beaded brow, as she replied, "I'm sure it can't be that. Nobody's been vomiting black bile, even in the last stages. It's more like the classic ague, or malaria, save for the fact that quinine sulfate seems to have no effect at all. I'll know better as soon as I finish here and administer some quinine I know to be the real McCoy."

Longarm didn't ask any dumb questions. She'd said she'd gotten the medicine she'd been giving them from government medical stores. But on the other hand, he'd arrested more than one son of a bitch for cheating the taxpayers with worthless drugs and inedible Indian rations.

Before he could ask any brighter questions, the sheeting parted and a blandly pretty gal, wearing too much face paint and red hair Mother Nature had never issued her, popped in, the butcher's apron over her blue calico summer frock smeared with all sorts of crud. She sobbed at old Norma, "I think that poor boy from the Coast Guard station must be dead, Doctor Richards!"

Norma went on stitching as she muttered something to herself, and then asked Longarm, "Would you know, and could you make sure for us, Custis? As you see, I only have four arms."

Longarm allowed he'd seen a few dead folks in his time, and followed the mock redhead outside. As they passed the cluster of worried Mexican folks, he assured them in Spanish their Papacito was doing just fine. The older daughter still tagged along as he followed the fancy nursing sister across the cavernous icehouse between the rows of close-packed cots.

The Mexican gal made the sign of the cross as they approached a sad scene against the far wall. Two more nurses in fancy clothes were gathered over a nice-looking half-naked corpse. There was no mistaking unconscious from dead once a person's nose turned to wax like that. As he joined the gals over the dead Coast Guardsman, Longarm declared, "At least a couple of hours. You'd best cover his face, ladies. He wouldn't want us looking at him as he commences to stiffen."

One of the gals sobbed, "He was ever so nice, even when the ague was on him, and I feel so awful about not looking at him sooner. But we thought he was asleep!"

Longarm said soothingly, "I doubt there's much any of you ladies could have done for him had you noticed sooner. No offense, but are you ladies volunteers from town?"

The three Anglo gals exchanged blushing glances. Only one burst out laughing. To cover up, the mock redhead asked, "Is rigor mortis when they get that silly grin on their dead faces, Doctor?"

Longarm grinned sort of silly himself, and replied, "I ain't no sawbones. I'm a federal marshal and, like you all, just helping out as best I know how. That wild mirthless smile you just mentioned is only part of what's called rigor mortis. It commences three to six hours after death, and you'll doubtless be glad to know they go limp and peaceful again in less than seventy-two. I have to know about such things in my line of work because sometimes it helps if we can make some educated guesses as to when somebody was killed."

He had no call to unsettle gals further with remarks about bloating, funny colors, or blowfly maggots. It made more sense to see if Norma Richards wanted the poor cuss buried before anything like that took place around here.

He said he'd tell her for them, and headed back across the icehouse. That Mexican gal in white cotton frills was still with him, which seemed reasonable seeing her kin were all gathered along that far side. He found her less reasonable when she asked him, in Spanish, if he had any notion what those painted and fancy-dressed Anglo gals really were.

He answered severely, "At the moment they seem to be acting as the only medical staff under the one professional in this improvised fever ward. The respected physicians and no doubt a lot of the other respectable citizens of this town have all run away like rabbits. So why don't we just call those braver women nurses for now, and save ourselves the worry of what they might or might not do for a living on other occasions?"

She blushed but didn't answer, or back down as far as he could tell, as they passed a sweat-soaked form in a bed croaking, *"Agua, por favor. Estoy mareado. Pero no puedo dormir."*

Longarm nodded and told the Mexican gal, "There you go. Those ladies you've been low-rating might not know this gent's asking for a drink of water, and could likely need more help than that right now. I'll go tell Doc Richards he's feeling dizzy and restless. Why don't you go back and tell them other gals he needs some water *poco tiempo*?"

She said she would. Longarm continued on past her kin with a nod, ducked back inside, and said, "That redhead was right about the Coast Guardsman. There's a Mex out yonder croaking for water and complaining he's too dizzy to get up and too restless to lie down. What do you want me to do for him, Doc?"

She went on bandaging the groggy Mexican farmer's knee as she replied, "I could use some help with that heavy Saratoga, Custis. But once it's in here I can manage, if I'm right about the quinine sulfate."

As he turned to go he heard her murmur, "If I'm wrong, I don't know what I'll do."

Longarm ducked out into the bright morning sunlight, half blinded but surprised at how cool it felt next to that steamy stink inside. South Texas did tend to stay pleasant for a few days after a nasty storm. The air smelled more of sea foam than mosquito swamp right now. He wondered if that was going to rid Escondrijo of this fever outbreak. Sometimes a change in the weather helped. Sometimes it didn't. He wasn't packing a badge to worry about such matters all that much.

He untethered the mules and led them, along with the wagon, around to the slot of shade between the icehouse and a smaller warehouse to its north, explaining, "We were in a hurry with that gator victim, *amigos*. I know you're both anxious to get out of those traces and put yourselves around some fodder and water. I'll be dropping you off at the address La Bruja gave me in just a few more minutes. So just bear with me till I tote old Norma's trunk inside and find out where she's stored my own shit, hear?"

Neither brute was in any position to argue as he tethered them again, reset the wagon brake, and slid the heavy trunk out the back of the wagon box.

As he carried it back inside on his back, the older of the Mexican kids came to join him, offering to help. So Longarm let him. Aside from not wanting to show off, he didn't want to insult a *macho* ten-year-old by implying he needed no help from such a squirt.

So, between them, they had the Saratoga trunk over by old Norma about the time she'd slid some of the sheeting out of the way to let everyone else at Papacito. The mangled Mexican was sitting up, though a mite green around the gills, as everyone said how brave he'd just been, unconscious or not.

The matronly Anglo doctor fell upon her trunk with ill-disguised glee, saying, "I know for a fact I packed fresh full-strength quinine sulfate among my other supplies. Lord knows how I'll get more, on such short notice, should that prove to be the answer."

Longarm suggested, "I could wire the Rangers in Corpus Christi for more medical supplies, seeing I got to wire in a progress report this morning in any case, Miss Norma."

She shook her head. "No, you can't. Did you think I was on my own like this because I enjoy sweating? The wires were swept away in that storm last night. I did get off one overly optimistic report when I first arrived. I had half as many fever victims to worry about and plenty of quinine to fight it with, so I thought!"

Longarm grimaced. "Didn't have all that many answers to wire Billy Vail yet anyways. I'd best carry that borrowed rig and team over where I promised I would. You can tell me about my own saddle and such when I come back from that and mayhaps a few other morning errands."

La Bruja had written down the name and address of a small chandler's shop down the quay from the regular steamer landing. With no steamers in port the quay was nearly deserted as Longarm drove along it, the mules clopping and wheels rolling crisply on the oak-block paving. There were a dozen-odd Mexican fishing luggers tied up at the south end, with some smaller cat boats hauled up on the mud just beyond. He found a row of modest Mexican-owned shops just south of the fair-sized brick-walled edifice that proclaimed itself a meat packer in big block letters. He'd expected a larger operation. The chandler shop a few doors down was modest as well. But as soon as one studied on it, neither an outfit shipping occasional cargos of cold-storage beef nor a chandler selling ship's stores to a mess of Mexican fishermen had to look as if they belonged in Chicago.

He got down and tethered the team to a hitching rail out front. He went on in to find the chandlery poorly lit, pungent with the odors of hemp, tar, and peppers, and presided over by a big fat Mexican with a pleasant smile and deliberately stupid attitude.

When Longarm introduced himself and allowed he had a rig and mule team belonging to La Bruja outside, the chandler looked confused and said, "You stole that wagon from some witch, you say, *señor*? Forgive me, I mean no disrespect, but you seem to have me confused with someone else. On the head of my children I know nothing of witches or stolen goods!"

Longarm said patiently, "They told me the wires were down and I don't want us endangering any kid's head. So what say I just leave that team and rig tied up out front, the way I promised La Bruja I might, and we'll just say no more about it?"

The chandler shrugged. "Is a free country, no? Who am I to say where an Anglo lawman parks his wagon along a public quay?"

Longarm allowed that sounded reasonable and, as long as he was there, offered to buy a box of those Mexican waterproof matches. But the fat chandler told him to just help himself to a box and go with God. So he did, certain he'd left El Bruja's property with someone smart enough to see she got it all back.

He strode over to the main street, a block inland, and asked some kids playing marbles in the still-damp street the way to their town lockup. They directed him to a brick building across from the white-washed Methodist steeple one could see for miles around.

As he strode the plank walk along the shady side of the street, he heard the kids behind him debating his station in life. They seemed divided as to whether he was a Ranger or simply some other pistol-packer with business at the town lockup.

Longarm had been a kid one time. So when one of then announced he'd just ask and jumped up to chase after him, Longarm stopped and turned with an indulgent smile.

But then his smile froze as a distant shot rang out and the kid caught a bullet aimed at Longarm's spine with the back of his poor little head!

Longarm's own gun was out and he was already running as the kid who'd taken a bullet for him beat a heavy mist of blood and brain tissue to the boardwalk with his small dead face. Longarm yelled at the other kids to get down and stay down as he tore past. The dirty white cloud of gunsmoke he'd spotted still hung shoulder-high near the corner he'd just turned. It was easy to see some son of a bitch had trailed him from the more open waterfront and pegged a backshot down this other street from cover.

Before Longarm could run that far he heard the receding hoofbeats of a rapid mount. But he still caught a glimpse of a roan rump and a rider wearing an ankle-length duster of tan linen under his gray Texas hat as he tore around yet another corner with Longarm bawling after him, "Stand and fight like a human being, you yellow-bellied baby-butchering backshooting bastard!"

Then, sick at heart at that butchered kid, Longarm had to turn around and see if there was anything he could do to help.

There wasn't much. A crowd had already gathered and the dead kid's young mother, a careworn dishwater-blonde, had already dashed from her quarters nearby to cradle her child's shattered skull in her lap, oblivious of the mess it was making of her thin calico dress as she rocked mindlessly on her knees, assuring him it wasn't his fault and nobody was going to give him a licking this time.

Just beyond her, a copper badge and drawn .45 were staring at Longarm thoughtfully. So Longarm lowered his own .44–40 to his side and quickly called out, "I'm the law too. Federal. We're after a killer in a tan duster and gray Texas hat, mounted on a roan. Last seen headed south along that dirt path past those fishing boats along the lagoon."

The town law, an older as well as shorter Texican with a walrus mustache, with his badge riding the buttoned black vest over a crisp white shirt and shoestring tie, called back, "Lucky for you others further down the street at the time tell the same story. So who are you and why was that warmly dressed rascal out to backshoot you?"

To which Longarm could only reply, "I'd be U.S. Deputy Marshal Custis Long. I don't know the answers to your other questions yet. But I sure aim to find out!"

Chapter 8

A long time passed slowly by as Longarm and the local law did their best to restore some damned law and order in the middle of Escondrijo. They got the dead boy to the undertaker's, and got statements backing Longarm's from the kids he'd been playing marbles with that morning. Constable W.R. Purvis decided, and Longarm was inclined to agree, it might be best in this climate to have the dead kid tidied up and embalmed ahead of any formal findings by the county coroner, who was busy enough with that fever going round.

Purvis had to reason harder before Longarm reluctantly agreed that a posse's chances of tracking a dimly described rider on a public trail would be too slim to justify the excitement. Longarm had already considered the possibility of that bastard discarding the duster and flashy hat before simply holing up on a nearby spread, or even back in town afoot after sending his pony on alone.

It was a trick as old as riding the owlhoot trail for fun and profit with pistol or, hell, rapier. Horses were something like homing pigeons when it came to heading back to a familiar stall, where a critter could laze secure from surprises while being well watered and fed. Horses hated surprises, which was why they could spook over something innocent as a tumbleweed, or run back into a burning stable bewildered by all the excitement and seeking familiar shelter from such a confusing world. And so, as the older town law man pointed out, that backshooter and his mount could be most anywhere by now, whether still together or far apart. When Longarm asked how many roan ponies there might be around Escondrijo, old W.R. shrugged and asked, "Would you like a list of riders alphabetic or numerical, assuming me and all the folks I'd have to check with ain't missed none? This is *cattle country*, pard. Save for townies and Mex hoe farmers close to town, most everyone for miles around rides *some* damned sort of horse, and roan ain't an unusual color for a cow pony. Was it a strawberry roan or a blue roan, by the way?"

Longarm grunted, "Strawberry." W.R. was too polite to tell an obvious horseman that that particular mixture of longer white guard hairs over a basic hide of auburn was ten times more likely to occur than the white over black they called a blue roan.

By the time they got down to the reasons Longarm had been headed to see Constable Purvis in the first place, they were entering the town lockup, where Purvis allowed he had a jar of corn squeezings filed under R, for Refreshments.

As Longarm's eyes adjusted to the sudden gloom, he saw they had no current customers in the three holding cells along the back wall.

As the lawman who ran the place got the jar and a couple of shot glasses from his filing cabinet, motioning Longarm to one of the bentwood chairs between the desk and a gun rack, he explained how both Deputy Gilbert and that federal want, Clay Baldwin, were out at that Coast Guard station to the north of town now.

Handing Longarm a perilously generous drink, Purvis continued. "They've both been taking turns, like everyone else, with that off-and-on-again fever. Seems every time your prisoner was well enough your deputy took sick, and vice versa. Young Gilbert told us someone like you would be coming, and meanwhile he felt he'd be able to hold Baldwin more secure in the Coast Guard brig whilst he lay sick or not so sick in their dispensary out yonder."

As they clinked, drank up, and gaped in mutual agony, the older lawman recovered his voice first. "If you ask me, your man is full of shit. We was holding Baldwin secure enough here. Why do you reckon he felt them Coast Guardsmen would be better at it?"

Longarm's tongue still felt numb, that corn liquor running close to two hundred proof, but he still managed to reply, "I don't know. I mean to ask him. I'd have thought both of 'em would be under the care of that lady doctor, Norma Richards, here in town. I just saw the cadaver of the pharmacist's mate they say was in charge out at that Coast Guard station."

Constable Purvis took a more cautious sip and replied, "We heard he'd come down with it too. I reckon it's the patent cell they got out yonder that's admired so much by young Gilbert. It wasn't that dead Coast Guardsman who was treating your deputy and your prisoner. That bossy sawbones you just mentioned has commandeered quarters out to the Coast Guard station, her being some sort of federal personage too fancy for the one hotel in town, and the Coast Guard station only standing a mile outside of town."

"You mean she rides back and forth between that federal post and her fever ward here in town?" Longarm asked before he'd had time to consider the obvious reasons.

Since he had, he was already back on his feet and saying something about having many another chore ahead before everyone who could holed up for *la siesta*. So Constable Purvis never got to fully explain how tough it might be to squeeze a whole town's worth of fever victims into the officers' quarters out at that Coast Guard station.

First things coming first, Longarm retraced his steps to that Mexican-owned chandlery on the waterfront. He wasn't surprised to see the team and rig he'd borrowed from La Bruja no longer stood out front.

When he went inside, he wasn't surprised to hear the fat chandler deny any knowledge of the propery El Señor had left outside his door of his own free gringo will.

Longarm said, "I ain't worried about La Bruja getting her

property back one way or another if you know what's good for you. I've come back to talk about some gunplay just up your side street. I reckon you never noticed that neither?"

The chandler shrugged his fat shoulders and replied he'd heard the shots, and that someone had told him an Anglo *muchacho* had been murdered by some person or persons unknown. When he added he paid little attention to such matters, since *los gringos* always seemed to be fighting among themselves, Longarm muttered, "Touché. Now why don't we try her another way. How are you called, *amigo*?"

The fat man smiled coldly and replied, "Gomez. For some reason a lot of my customers call me Gordo Gomez. I reserve the right to say whether I am anyone's *amigo* or not."

Since Gordo translated almost literally as "Fatso," Longarm felt free to call him that whether they were to be pals or not. He smiled thinly at the fat Mexican and said, "*Bueno, Gordo mio*. The *pendejo* who shot that kid in the head not far from here was aiming at my back. He fired from cover after trailing me as far as the main street from guess where?"

Gordo returned his stare innocently and replied, "Not from here, if that is what you mean."

Longarm said, "That's exactly what I mean. I hadn't told a soul in town I was coming your way with La Bruja's rig and mule team. So how do you reckon that backshooter knew just where to wait for me?"

Gordo shrugged and sounded sincerely innocent as he simply asked, "*Quien sabe*? El Señor was openly driving through town in a vehicle even he describes as the property of some witch, no?"

Longarm started to object, saw he had no sensible objection to the fat man's simple logic, and said, "*Mierditas*, you could have a point. La Bruja told me herself she'd been approached by someone who wanted me dead. It stands to reason anyone apt to plot murder with a lady might know her mules and covered box-wagon on sight!"

Gordo stared up at a strip of fly paper as if debating with himself whether to change it for a fresh one as he told Longarm in the same politely firm tone he had no idea what they were talking about.

So Longarm nodded, suggested Gordo cut down on sweets at least, and headed back up the quay toward old Norma's improvised fever ward, his spine feeling itchy even though he kept looking behind him all the way.

Nobody seemed out for a second crack at him, and so he made it to the icehouse without further incident.

Inside, he found the Mexican farmer he'd brought in holding court on a corner cot, surrounded by other admiring farm folks as well as the kin who'd come in with him. It seemed that while alligators weren't unheard of along the Fever Coast, man-eating alligators were rare indeed.

He found the farmer's slim young daughter on the far side of the icehouse, translating for Norma Richards as the two of them tried to dose a flushed and sweaty Mexican kid with quinine sulfate. Longarm knew how bitter the shit-brown pills tasted. But it was the motherly Norma who decided, "Oh, fiddle, just give him ice water, Consuela. Lord knows this stuff doesn't seem to be helping any of the others, and the poor boy's sick enough without a broken jaw!"

She spotted Longarm and straightened up, saying wearily, "We heard about the shooting, Custis. You certainly do lead a very interesting life!"

Longarm sighed and said, "So do you, Miss Norma. You say quinine don't seem to work, even when you're sure it's real?"

She shook her head, brushed that same loose strand from her brow with the back of her hand, and explained. "We have to give the poor dears *something*. My sweet young volunteer here thinks we ought to call in some witch doctors she knows, and you've no idea how tempting that seems as this day wears on. Lord knows, I may as well be dancing naked in paint and shaking a rattle for all the good I've been able to do anyone!"

Longarm had to chuckle at the picture. Old Norma was sort of what you might call Junoesque, if not pleasantly plump. But he assured the worried-looking gal, "Just getting 'em in bed out of the noonday sun must be helping 'em some, Miss Norma, and as for the *curados* Miss Consuela here might have mentioned, you can't exactly call a *curado* a witch doctor. They got the same sort of witches we worry about. They call 'em *brujas*. A *curado* or curer is more like a herbalist mixed with a Pentacostal preacher. Picture a Holy Roller speaking in tongues and casting out demons whilst dosing sick folks with sassafras bark, licorice root, and such. I know you'll find this hard to believe, Doc. But that very quinine you've been dosing these folks with was discovered by Indian medicine men. I once read about a highborn Spanish lady being saved on her deathbed by some Jesuit missionary back from the woods with some bitter bark the Indians had given him."

She nodded and said, "The Countess Chinchon, who introduced it to Europe as Peruvian bark around 1640. You're so right about a weak brew of ground-up tree bark saving her life and restoring her to almost perfect health. So why don't these patients respond to pure quinine sulfate, more than ten times as strong?"

Longarm suggested, "They have another fever entirely, ma'am. I'd forgot the name of that countess. But I read somewhere that the stuff only works on one particular family of fevers. I know for a fact you can't cure yellow jack with quinine."

She nodded but insisted, "This fever here is nothing at all like yellow jack, and please give me credit for reading a little myself!"

She swept a bare arm rather grandly around at the sweltering icehouse. "They've all been suffering the same symptoms. They're hit without warning by a sudden violent rise in temperature, along with headaches, muscular cramps, and drenching sweats."

Longarm shrugged and said lots of fevers did that to folks.

She snapped, "I hadn't finished! The patient is helped by liquids but can barely tolerate broths. The poor appetite is complicated by an almost suicidal depression. Then, as suddenly as it began, or after a bout of chills and shivering, the patient suddenly snaps out of it, save for feeling weak, dehydrated, and ravenously hungry."

Longarm allowed, "That sure sounds like plain old ague. Chills, fever, and you say it comes back?"

She nodded, repressed a shiver of her own, and told him, "It's usually the second or third attack that takes them. I don't know if it's because the fever gets stronger or hits them the same way once they're weaker. We know so little, Custis, for all our Latin terms and impressive diplomas!"

Longarm suddenly found himself holding the sort of solid old gal against his chest, smoothing her brown hair with a gentle free hand as he said, "Don't go blubbering up on us now. These sick folks are depending on you, whether you know what you're doing here or not. Ain't it possible the bugs that cause the ague can get used to quinine the way those Austrian miners I've read about get used to arsenic?"

She leaned against him, sort of like a babe lost in the woods might have. But her voice was cheerful enough as she marveled, "My, you *do* seem to read a lot, don't you?"

To which he could only modestly reply, "They got a fine public library up in Denver, and along about the end of the month I ain't got the money to spend my free evenings at the opera. Could we discuss these invisible bugs instead of my modest wages, ma'am?"

She sighed and said, "I work for the same cheap government. I've already considered a strain of a still-unknown microbe building up a resistance to the usual specific drug. That could be the answer, or just as cheerfully, you could be right about it being some entirely different malady and . . . Oh, Custis, I'm so *tired,* even if I knew what I was doing!"

He said, "At least you've been trying, and that has to count for something. I understand you've been treating others out at that Coast Guard station you're staying at?"

She sounded half asleep as she replied, "A Deputy Gilbert, that prisoner called Baldwin, and one of the officers, an Ensign Dorfler. For some reason the garrison out there's been lighty hit by whatever this may be. Everyone out there who's suffered any fever at all came down with it here in town, or shortly after returning to the garrison from town."

She didn't seem to be getting any lighter on her feet as he kept on holding her there near the grinning Mexican kid. So Longarm reached up to remove his Stetson and wave it some for attention as he asked the big gal in his other arm whether his McClellan and Winchester might be out at that Coast Guard station as well.

She murmured, "In my quarters near the dispensary. You had all my toiletries with you in that trunk, so I had to use some soap from one of your saddlebags and I hope you don't . . ."

Then she was fast asleep against his shirtfront, and he had to put his hat back on and grab her with both arms as her knees went to sleep down yonder as well.

The gal with the mock red hair came over to join them, looking scared as she asked Longarm, "What's wrong? Don't tell me she's down with it too!"

Longarm didn't. He said, "I suspect she's just run herself into the ground. If you'd help me find a place to lay her down and stretch her out, it's going on siesta time in any case and I got to get on out to that Coast Guard station."

The gal nodded and said, "There's a lie-down we've been taking turns with over by the autopsy theater. That's what Doctor Norma calls the corner she uses to cut 'em open, dead or alive, the autopsy theater."

Longarm nodded, scooped the semi-conscious Norma up in both arms as if he were toting someone's mighty big baby off to bed, and let the other gal lead the way.

Their progress didn't go unnoticed by all the other volunteers. So there were others around them as Longarm lay the exhausted Norma on the semi-secluded cot in a shadowy nook between those hanging sheets and the brick wall of the improvised fever ward.

As he straightened up, Longarm observed, "She'd do better out of that starched-linen outfit with just a thin sheet over her. But I'd best let you ladies worry about that after I leave, right?"

93

One of the other gals, a small bleached blonde, suddenly covered her face and bawled, "I can't stand this! I can't
tell whether these government folk are trying to be polite or
mocking!"

The red-haired gal told the bemused Longarm, "Tess ain't
used to being called a lady. None of us are. But you're trying
to be a good sport, right?"

Longarm shook his head. "Nope. Calling 'em as I see 'em.
Lots of folks who call themselves ladies and gents have run
off and left those sick folks you've been caring for to die."

The mock redhead shrugged and said, "Business was slow
with a damned plague keeping all the cowhands out of town in
any case. I know you think we're stupid as well as low-down,
Deputy Long, but hell, no girl with a lick of sense would be
in our usual line of work to begin with."

Longarm said, "My friends call me Custis. Maybe it takes
a lady with a foolish but generous nature to act the way all of
you have been acting. I could tell you a tale of another swell
gal they named a mountain after up Colorado way. But I got
to be on my way now. So some other time."

The gal tagged after him. "*My* friends call me Ruby. How did
you say you meant to get out to that Coast Guard station . . .
Custis?"

He said, "On foot, I reckon. They say it's only a mile and
these low-heeled boots I wear were bought with such dismal
events in mind."

Ruby said, "I have my own shay and a high-stepping trotter
over to the livery, if you're not ashamed to be seen in broad
day with a lady of the evening."

Longarm started to ask about old Norma. But the other gals
seemed to have that under control. So he grinned at Ruby and
declared, "You're on. But there are gossips up in Denver who
might say it was you who was risking her reputation in the
company of such a wicked rascal, ma'am."

Chapter 9

By then it was almost as hot outside, although sweeter-smelling, and the streets were nearly deserted as *la siesta* set in, with a heap of local Anglos participating. You had to go north to somewhat cooler parts of Texas to hear folks talking about lazy greasers in the noonday sun. The folks who'd been in the Great Southwest longer were as willing to work, when they had to, as most. But south of, say, San Antone, you knocked off a few hours from about noon to four in the afternoon, unless you felt like frying eggs on your skull with the help of that subtropical sun. Mexicans tended to sneer at lazy gringo shopkeepers who knocked off for the day before midnight, when anyone could see it was easier to go shopping after sundown. They themselves liked to finish their day's work around nine, dine late, and party till it got cool enough to make serious love after midnight. Going home for a snack, a quick screw, and a long nap during the daylight siesta made for a nice break.

So Longarm wasn't at all surprised when they found the livery across the way had closed for *la siesta*. He led Ruby in her sunbonnet around to the shady side, got out his pocketknife, and told her he'd whistle for her once he'd picked the front lock.

It didn't take long. They'd locked up more with kids in mind than serious horse thieves. So he whistled the friendly fancy gal inside, and took her word on which two-wheel shay was her own in the back. Once she'd introduced him to her frisky chestnut gelding with white stockings, he asked her if she wanted to find and fetch her own harness from the nearby tack room as he played Chinaman with the shay.

She said she would. So they parted friendly, and it only took him a few moments to get between the carriage shafts like some rickshaw coolie and haul the shay as far as that gelding's stall.

Ruby met him there empty-handed, whispering, "I think there's a dead man in the tack room!"

He told her it was likely just one of the stable hands, but drew his six-gun as he led the way through the low overhang between the stalls and tack room.

He had to chuckle as he saw at a glance he'd been right. There was no way to tell what the Mexican propped up on his rump in a corner looked like. He'd wrapped up in his striped wool serape and pulled his big straw sombrero down over his sleepy face. But when you took a longer look you could see he was breathing, while the little brown jug of *pulque* on its side beside him suggested it might be a waste of time to try and wake him.

So Longarm asked Ruby which horse collar and harness went with her shay, and wasn't surprised when she picked a well-blackened and silver-mounted outfit. Her shay had hard rubber wheel rims too.

As he harnessed the bay in its stall before backing it out, Ruby made a snooty comment on the way greasers dozed off at the dangedest times and places. He didn't waste time defending honest working folk to even a good-natured whore till Ruby asked, as if she really cared, "How come they like to sleep sitting up that way? You see them all over town propped up against a wall in a blanket with their hats down over their faces."

As he harnessed the bay between her carriage shafts and paid its four ribbons back through her silver-plated fittings, he told her, "It ain't as if anyone *likes* to sleep sitting up. But it beats trying to get comfortable lying down on hard dirt or the softest planking. I've found I wake up less stiff, after a long

96

night on a cross-country train, if I shoot for my forty winks sitting up. They sleep flat as the rest of us when they've got a softer bed to lay flat on, Miss Ruby."

She smiled at him sassily and allowed she felt sure he knew all about sleeping with all sorts of folks in all sorts of odd positions. But he didn't brag about any Mexican gals he'd been to bed with as he led the frisky pony and its sassy owner out of the livery.

He put up the shay's folding top against the overhead sun before he helped her up to the cozy seat. He handed her the ribbons, and got out his knife to politely lock the livery door again. When he climbed up beside the mock redhead, he discovered the seat to be cozier than he'd expected. Ruby's rump was either wider than he'd judged it to be under her flouncy calico skirts, or she'd slid it to her right as he got in on that side.

There was no discussion as to who was to drive. No man was about to sit back and let a woman drive him about as if she were his coach servant. So she handed him the ribbons without him having to ask, but told him which way to go as he clucked his tongue at the bay and lightly flipped its big brown rump with some slack in the ribbons. As they lit out and he let the pent-up pony stretch its legs in a handsome trot, he assured its owner he knew north from south. "I suspect I was on the regular coast road last night. It was flooded in some stretches by that gale and I had to swing way inland but . . . Lord have mercy, was it only last night I was driving down the other way? It feels like at least three days. I can generally stay up a good seventy-two hours before I feel *this* tired. Reckon it's all the excitement since I got into Escondrijo this morning. But once I settle a few things out to that Coast Guard post I might be able to catch my own siesta."

She said, "It's not too late to turn back, if you'd really like a nice long nap in the nice soft bed in my private quarters."

He chuckled and declined her kind offer with a gallant observation about just how much sleep a man might get amid such exciting surroundings.

She didn't answer for a time as they trotted on out the north end of the tiny town. When she did, she sighed and said, "I see you drive with a firm but gentle hand, Custis. You're allowing Chocolate to set his own pace, but we all know exactly who's in command of this expedition, right?"

He shrugged and replied, "I've never held with being harder than I need to be with a critter taking me the way I wanted to go in the first place, ma'am."

Ruby nodded. "So I've noticed. Even some of the purer folks we've been trying to help back there in that icehouse haven't been able to resist comical comments about Doc Richards' nursing staff. But you called us ladies and acted as if we were, until I as much as told you right out that I liked you!"

He said, "I like you too, Miss Ruby, and I mean that sincerely. I never said I didn't want to go to bed with you. I only said I had a mess of chores to tend to."

She said, "I'll bet. I just said I admired the polite way you got exactly where you wanted to go, with no straying from your very own determined course. Did you think I was inviting you up to one of the cribs in the . . . hotel I usually work in?"

He shook his head and said, "I know all sorts of ladies like to keep their own private notions in their very own quarters, ma'am. I ain't all that pure. I've made all sorts of friends along the way, and one of 'em was that very Colorado gal of easy virtue I was speaking of back yonder. They called her Silver Heels up in hardrock country. Some say she was a miner's young widow, whilst others say she wound up doing what she had to do because some worthless rascal ran off and left her stranded in a mountain mining camp."

Ruby leaned closer, as if someone might overhear her above the the clopping hoofbeats in the middle of a deserted street, as she told Longarm, "She was either out to punish herself, or punish some man who'd betrayed her former true nature, or she just plain liked it. Nobody can turn a gal wicked against her will, no matter how she might lie to you men afterwards."

Longarm noticed some thoughtful souls, likely old-time Mexicans, had planted cottonwood, or alamo as they called it, along either side of the wagon trace outside of town. Cottonwood grew fast, but he figured it had been planted a while back, judging by how the fluttering leaves of the overhead branches shaded clean across the road in places while providing at least dappled sunlight most everywhere else. He really liked thoughtful souls. So thinking back to how a soiled dove called Silver Heels had turned out, he told Ruby the bittersweet story of a sister in sin as they drove on through the uncertain light.

Silver Heels, so called for the silver heels of her dancing shoes because she refused to give her real name, had been making money hand over fist as the prettiest and some said friskiest whore in a mining camp that varied some with the teller of the tale. But everyone who told it, one way or another, agreed it was smallpox, breaking out in mid-winter when the trails were closed, that made things get grim as all hell. Some said there was no doc in town at all. Others said there might have been, but not unlike Norma Richards, he'd been overwhelmed by the plague, and so Silver Heels had pitched in alone to help. In either case, it had been that one lone whore, working round the clock serving soup and cleaning the fevered, pussy bodies of half the folks in camp, who'd saved the fifty or sixty percent who'd come through alive. So later on, the grateful miners had picked out a particularly pretty peak and named it Mount Silver Heels. Longarm assured this other good-natured whore, "There's no doubt about where Mount Silver Heels is today. You can find it on any large-scale map of Colorado."

"Where might the real Silver Heels be found today?" asked Ruby in a pensive tone.

Longarm shrugged. "Nobody knows. She just left the hardrock country with the smallpox and the next spring thaw. You hear some say she had to quit whoring because her pretty little face had been scarred up hideously by the pox she caught helping so many others fight off. Others say she married a miner who'd struck it so rich he could afford to keep her and her frisky favors all to himself. I've even heard tell that today the former Silver Heels is a respectable and highly respected young matron of Denver's high society."

"What's the truth, Custis?" Ruby asked, as if she felt sure he'd know.

He did, and it was a sin to lie when you didn't have to. So he told her, "Let's just say her story had an ending a lady asked me not to tell anyone else. My point was that a nice gal is a nice gal, no matter what others may think of her."

Ruby told him he was awfully nice too, and snuggled closer as Longarm drove on through the dotted line of sunlight and shadows. When he suddenly reined in, Ruby sat up with a start to gaze all about and ask why. They'd passed the last corn *milpas* north of town, and the tree-shaded wagon trace was surrounded by spartina reeds to seaward and thickets of gumbo-limbo saplings on the higher ground to their left. When Ruby asked why they'd stopped, pointing out the Coast Guard station was almost in sight ahead, Longarm told her, "I know where we are. You could doubtless see the station from here if it wasn't for all those cottonwoods and the way this wagon trace curves just enough to follow the natural lay of the land. I'm a lot more concerned about the way we've just come. I thought I heard some other hoofbeats behind us. But when I reined in just now, somebody else might have too!"

She leaned out her side to peer back around the oilcloth cover, saying, "I don't see anybody, Custis. Even if I did, this is hardly a private road, is it?"

To which he replied more soberly, "Innocent travelers on a public thoroughfare don't stop at least two furlongs back when someone out ahead reins in. So let's see if we can skin this cat some other way."

She assumed they were going on to the nearby Coast Guard station when Longarm clucked the bay forward some more but kept a tighter hold on the ribbons to just walk them along the wagon trace a ways. Then, leaning out his own side first, he swung them off through the rank Bermuda grass between the cottonwood boles, apparently heading right at a solid wall of close-packed saplings.

She said, "Chocolate can't pull us through that tangle of second growth, Custis!"

He said, "I know. It ain't second growth. Gumbo-limbo never grows much bigger. It can't make up its mind whether it's a big bush or a small tree. Meanwhile, that ain't exactly where I'm heading."

Ruby grabbed hold of the top braces on her side as he suddenly swung them broadside to the wagon trace, headed back the way they'd just come. He was as surprised as she was by the unexpected gap in the gumbo-limbo they almost passed. But he still reined in and backed them into it before handing her the reins and saying, "Hold on whilst I shut the door."

So she did as Longarm slid between the carriage poles and the slick thin trunks of gumbo-limbo to ease back out in the open and, spotting nobody else in sight, quickly cut and gather a big light but awkward bundle of sea grape.

Sea grape wasn't related to real grapes. Folks called the seaside bush growing all along the gulf coast that because its big thick leaves looked remotely like grape leaves. Left to itself, the stuff seldom grew shoulder high. But Longarm was able to pile his severed sea grape canes in the opening he'd found in the gumbo-limbo to where somebody passing on the nearby wagon trace might dismiss the small hideout as something that just wasn't worth reining in to study.

He took the ribbons back from Ruby, gave the bay enough slack to lower its muzzle to the lush bluestem growing in the shady slot, then lowered the shay's oilcoth top as he explained, "I left us just enough room to watch yon wagon trace over the tops of that piled brush. I want anybody coming along now to have to guess where even the tops of our heads might be."

She didn't complain. It was just as shady under the gumbo-limbo branches arching overhead. She took off her sunbonnet and shook out her long dyed hair, saying, "I hope nobody ever comes along. It's so cool and, well . . . romantic in this little nook you found for us, you devil."

He removed his own hat to break up the pattern someone tailing them might be watching for. It was no accident that the Indians made the hand sign for a white man by holding a stiff palm across their brow. Currier and Ives would have it that the Indians with their hands like that were shading their eyes as they peered off in the distance for white folks. Folks who knew Indians better knew any Indian holding his hand like so had already spotted white folks. The way a white rider's hat brim divided his head between light and shadow was more obvious at a distance.

They sat hatless for a long time, and nothing seemed to be taking place on the wagon trace. Longarm was dying for some sleep or a smoke, in that order. Since neither seemed safe just then he said, "They must have figured where I was headed and fell back when I spooked 'em by reining in, as if I'd spotted 'em."

She sniffed and asked if he might not be taking a lot for granted, adding she was used to being followed some herself.

Longarm chuckled at the picture and assured her, "I'm sure I see why, Miss Ruby. But no offense, I figure the odds on a crook trailing me are greater than those for an admirer trailing a lady with an armed escort. To begin with, there's been a lot of such sinister trailing going on of late."

Since she seemed to care, he brought her up to date on his recent brushes with sinister strangers, having no call to hold back all that much. For as he'd told La Bruja around this time the day before, they hadn't sent him on any secret mission.

Once he'd told Ruby what he had been sent down this way to tend to, she said, "You're right. It's mysterious as hell. If someone was out to rescue that outlaw you were sent to fetch, wouldn't they do better going after the lawmen holding him before you ever got here?"

He repressed a yawn and said, "That's about the size of it. Marshal Vail never sent me down here to pester anybody else, and the Rangers in Corpus Christi agreed the two gunslicks I can account for by name ain't wanted state or federal. Not by *those* names, at any rate. So I'd say the mysterious mastermind offering money to have me backshot has a mighty uneasy conscience and suspects I'm really on to him."

This time he couldn't help from yawning as he added, "I sure wish I knew what I'm supposed to have on him. So far two innocent bystanders, another nice gal and an innocent kid, have stopped bullets meant for me, and I'm commencing to feel mighty vexed!"

Ruby said, "I can see how anyone would. Tell me more about that Mex whore, La Bruja. You say she admitted she'd been offered money to do you dirty, Custis?"

He nodded but said, "*Bruja* stands for witch, not whore, and you might say she's more a doxy or outlaw gal than either. I suspect she operates something like an Anglo gal called Belle Starr, up north in the Cherokee Strip near Fort Smith. Gents on the dodge need places to stay, store their ill-gotten gains, and mayhaps swap mounts betwixt owlhoot adventures. Had La Bruja and her own gang wanted to do me dirt for that bounty on my fool head, she'd have had no call to tell me all about it and help me slip out of town on the sneak after dark, right?"

Ruby shrugged and replied, "I suppose not. What sort of a lay did you say this Mexican spitfire was, handsome?"

Longarm yawned some more and replied, "I never said. I never do. A man who'd talk dirty about a lady who's been nice to him would no doubt write dirty words on walls as well."

She insisted, "A lot of men do. I've been in the gents' room after visiting hours at my, ah . . . place of business. Is that why you'd rather fool with outlaw greaser gals than a white gal like me, Custis? I ain't been with a man since my last period, if that's what's stopping you!"

He laughed incredulously and declared, "For Pete's sake, we've pulled off the trail in broad daylight to find out who's been trailing us with possibly sinister intent!"

To which she demurely replied, "Pooh, nobody's coming on that old wagon trace, and I'd just love to come with you in this sweet old love nest you've brought me to, you big tease."

He fought back another yawn, knowing how cruel it might look to yawn at such a time, as he insisted, "There really was another pony trotting along under those infernal trees, Miss Ruby."

She began to unbotton her formfitting calico bodice as she said, "I'm not calling you a fibber. As I told you before, some of us are wicked because we want to punish ourselves, whilst others are wicked because they want it, a lot. I lost track of how many lovers I had on the side before I decided it made more sense to just leave my old husband and get paid for what I enjoyed most. The poor dear I married young was rich as well as horny enough, at first. But I fear I'm just too warm-natured to ever settle down with one man. Do you think that makes me some sort of a freak, Custis?"

He answered honestly, "If you're a freak you've got plenty of company, Miss Ruby, albeit few are quite as honest about feelings a lot of us seem to feel. I like to tell myself I can't stay true to one particular gal because of the tumbleweed job I have. On a couple of occasions when I nearly got caught I told myself, as well as the gal, that a man who packs a badge with my rep has no right to ask any lady to risk an early as well as likely widowhood, and I reckon I've really meant that more than once. But if the truth be told, I've always recovered from the wistful feeling of moving on."

She said she knew exactly what he meant, and added, "Let's get my lap robe out of the back and spread it on the grass in this sweet shade for some real sweet screwing!"

But he sighed and replied, "In tall, shaded grass, along the gulf coast after a rain, Miss Ruby? I can see you ain't been down this way long. They call 'em red bugs over near New Orleans and chiggers west of Galveston. By either name they bite like hell and itch way worse than mosquitos. There's one breed of red bug that burrows in under your nails and more delicate places to raise a rash that just won't quit. So take my advice and don't ever even spread a picnic blanket on the grass in a gumbo-limbo thicket, hear?"

Her form was popping out considerably now as she asked where, in that case, he wanted to screw her.

He gulped and started to point out he'd never asked to screw her anywhere. But he didn't want to sound like a sissy or, worse yet, a man who'd scorn a right nice-looking gal with one hell of a pair of naked tits. So he reeled her bare chest in against his thin shirt and kissed her on one ear as he muttered, "I've never found a better place than right betwixt a pretty lady's legs. But I hope it's understood I'd be aiding and abetting on duty if I was to offer money for any such favors."

She told him not to talk dirty, and added, "Does this one-horse shay look like a whorehouse, you stuck-up thing?"

So seeing she'd put it that way, he just peeled out of his own duds as she finished shucking her own, and laying her crossways on the leather seat with his own boots braced against a wheel and carriage shaft, stuck it to her as she thrust up to meet him, sobbing, "Oh, Lordy, just the way I like it! Just the way I needed it after washing off so many sick men's privates back there and not getting any for so many days and nights!"

He was glad he'd put his boots back on with just such purchase in mind. For there was much to be said for buggy riding when a man once got the hang of it, and as she gave it back to him with all the skill of a whore feeling really friendly, he surmised she'd done it in this very shay before.

But he never asked. It was her idea to note he acted as if he hadn't been in that Mexican gal after all. She was biting down hard with her innards as she husked, "You screw like a cowhand who's been out on the trail for months with nobody but his hand to put it in. Do you mind if I jerk my clit off whilst you prong me, honey? You do that so much better than your average horny cowhand, and I want to come a couple of times while I have your undivided attention!"

He grunted, "They asked the Prophet Mohammed about jerking off one time. He allowed he didn't see how it could be all that sinful, since nine out of ten folks did it and that tenth one was a liar."

So she laughed like a mean little kid, and slid her hand down between their bare bellies to strum her old banjo while Longarm shoved his own more sensitive parts as far up inside her as he could. So a great time was had by all, and when he asked Ruby how come she'd started crying at the end, she said it was because he'd kissed her on the mouth as she was coming. He started to say he never screwed anyone he found too disgusting to kiss. But upon reflection he felt that might sound sort of rude. So he just kissed her some more and confided he'd been coming too.

That inspired her to get on top, facing the other way so she could brace her high-buttoned heels on the floorboard and really bounce for him with her hands braced on her own knees while Longarm steadied her with a friendly grip on each bare hip. She allowed there was no need for her to strum herself anymore, now that he'd made her feel so womanly inside. He knew she was working harder to pleasure a pal when she peered back over her bare shoulder and confided, "As a rule I charge double to take it up my back door. But I'm not asking you for anything but . . . well, the nice way you treat a girl, if you want to shoot in my ass this time."

He'd been admiring the view of his love-slicked shaft going in and out of her regular entrance, which had light blond instead of mock red hair by the way. So he thrust up to meet a downstroke as he told her, "I'm doing fine, unless you really like it in your corn hole, honey."

She shook her mock red head and replied, "It doesn't feel good or bad back there, once you get it all the way in. I just knew some men to do that to a gal and, well, I like you, Custis!"

He said he liked her too just the way she was. So she giggled and commenced to really slide on up and down his old organ-grinder as he lay back and enjoyed her efforts. Poor old Lenore Colbert on that steamer coming north the other night had had ash-blond hair as well as a pussy she'd never really gotten to use like this. He found himself picturing that half-sated erection sliding in and out of that Boston virgin, and it felt pretty convincing with another gal's back to him as he rose to the occasion in her pussy with the light blond hair. But then Ruby shattered the illusion by declaring, "Oh, yes, I can tell you really like me and it makes me feel so grand to please you this way!"

Then she popped off, turned around, and swayed the shay under them alarmingly, before she dropped to her knees on the floorboards and kissed the turgid head of his aroused erection, cooing, "I want you to come where you weren't too proud to stick your tongue, darling!"

So he forgave her for not looking at all like the late Lenore as she proceeded to bob her mock red head up and down, taking him to the roots in a French sword swallow till he gasped "Jeeezusss!" and shot a wad he hadn't known he'd been saving somewhere on the far side of her tonsils.

He had to beg for mercy as she kept on swallowing, the rings of her deep throat rippling wetly up and down his shaft as she sucked every drop out of him.

So he was mighty tempted when she finally raised her head from his lap with a roguish grin, purring, "That was lovely. Would you like to take a nap with your head in Mamma's lap before we drive on? It's hot as hell out there right now, and you did say you hadn't had any sleep lately, didn't you?"

He reached for his boots, to take them off so he could put his jeans back on, saying, "Lord love you, Miss Ruby, I was already tired, and now I feel as if I could sleep for a month without getting up once to piss. But we'd best drive on anyways."

She sat straighter, stark naked above her garters, proud breasts heaving with emotion as she demanded, "Why? Don't you trust me not to betray you to the Philistines in your sleep?"

The thought had in fact occurred to him. He'd run into latter-day Delilahs before, and barely come out better than that other lawman, Samson, in the Good Book. But he just said he had to make sure his fellow deputy and their prisoner were all right before he lay his own head down for forty winks.

"You men are all alike!" she suddenly blazed. "I just took it in my mouth for you and you still think I'm a dirty bitch out to lift your wallet!"

When he said he thought no such thing, she demanded he prove it by laying his head right down in her lap or getting his ass right out of her private shay. So in the end, Longarm wound up walking the last couple of furlongs to that Coast Guard station to the north.

Chapter 10

He ran out of shade as the tree-lined wagon trace passed by the shell-paved cutoff leading across salt marsh and dune to the Coast Guard station they'd built on a finger of somewhat higher ground that pointed accusingly out to sea. As he approached the cluster of whitewashed frame buildings wrapped around a small parade ground, with a listless Revenue Service flag hanging high on its whitewashed staff, Longarm saw the place was smaller than he'd been expecting. It was about the size of a one-troop army outpost in Apacheria. There was nothing tied up to the one pier running out to deeper water in the coastal lagoon. So he wasn't surprised to see how quiet things were as he strode on to the gate in the four-strand bobwire perimeter. Aside from it being siesta time, a lot of the more important officers and men had to be out to sea aboard their steam cutter in the wake of that storm.

The U.S. Coast Guard was a branch of the Treasury Department instead of the Navy. But the sentry who challenged him at the gate wore a regular sailor suit of summer white with those leggings all sailors wore, for some reason, when they were ashore with rifles and cartridge belts. As Longarm showed the kid his badge and identification, he asked if those blamed leggings didn't itch in all this heat. The Coast Guardsman only sighed, and said he'd been told to expect someone from the Justice Department, adding Longarm would find the officer of the day at the headquarters building near the pier. Longarm didn't ask why they expected him to go there first.

It was considered polite as well as sensible to check in with the local law before you made any arrests in a strange town.

It felt like a day's forced march under that ferocious afternoon sun before he made it at last to the shady veranda running the full length of the freshly painted headquarters building. A junior grade lieutenant, equal to a first lieutenant in the army, came out of a doorway down the veranda in dress whites to tell Longarm they'd been starting to worry about him. As they shook hands, he introduced himself as a Lieutenant Junior Grade Devereaux, and said his boss, Lieutenant Flynn, was out chasing boys—or so it seemed to Longarm until he realized the young officer meant buoys, those floating markers they put out across the lagoon to show steamer pilots where to go.

As Devereaux led him inside Longarm remarked, "I can see how your C.O. would be anxious about channels and such after that storm along this coast. But that reminds me of something I was meaning to ask you all. Studying the map along my way up here from Brownsville, I noticed that big old Padre Island off to the east blocks this part of your big lagoon from the open gulf. So vessels putting in from the high seas can only enter the long lagoon well north of here."

The officer of the day motioned Longarm to a wicker chair by the big oak desk he was holding down for his superior and dinged a bell on it as he agreed. "Corpus Christi Pass. What's your question?"

Longarm replied, "What you're doing down here instead of up yonder, where you might be able to guard this big lagoon better, no offense."

Devereaux said, "None taken. You're not the first landsman who's asked me about that. We're not the Navy. We're the Coast Guard. Our mission here is to maintain channel buoys through a stretch of shifting grounds and watch for shifty smaller vessels than the Navy might be worried about. You've no idea how many places there are for smugglers or even pirates to put in along an almost deserted coast facing a monstrous sheltered lagoon!"

Longarm didn't have to answer for the moment as an orderly the lieutenant had obviously sent for refreshments when Longarm had been crossing the parade ground came in with a tray. As he put it on the desk and popped to attention, Longarm saw he'd brought a fifth of Bombay gin, a soda-water syphon, and a couple of tall glasses packed to their brims with chopped ice. Longarm didn't notice the small pill box before Devereaux dismissed the orderly and picked it up, saying "The British Navy's found it pays to stick to gin and tonic in the tropics. But quinine seems an acquired taste, so . . ."

"I only take medicine when I'm feeling poorly." Longarm said. "I ain't so sure about that ice either, this close to Old Mexico and the bellyaches that go with unboiled water down this way."

Devereaux smiled as he poured tall drinks, with and without the tonic, saying, "We get our ice at cost from Pryce & Doyle in town. They've assured us they boil all the water they put in their ice machine. As a matter of fact they furnish shops and even homes in Escondrijo with the clean modern ice they manufacture as a sideline to their meat packing."

Longarm reached for his own glass as he said, "I've seen their imposing packing plant. I'll take your word they know what they're up to down this way. What I really came out here to talk about was U.S. Deputy Marshall Gilbert and our federal prisoner, Clay Balwin. I understand you've got 'em both out here?"

Devereaux nodded. "Young Gilbert's in our sick bay, on orders of that federal germ chaser, Miss Richards. He seems to be feeling better, but Miss Richards says he's to stay in bed until she feels sure he won't run another fever, and she ought to know."

Longarm nodded, sipped the drink cautiously, tired as he already felt, and said, "I heard you've had some of that fever out this way as well. Where are you holding Baldwin, in your brig?"

Devereaux sounded reasonable as ever as he replied, "We've gotten off much lighter than they have in town. The skipper

111

thinks it might be because of our more healthful location. Baldwin's being held in solitary confinement on bread and water, pending your arrival."

That didn't sound so reasonable to Longarm. The tall deputy put his barely tasted drink down and rose to his considerable height as he grimly asked, "After a bout of a killing fever? Who ordered a diet of piss and punk for my sick prisoner?"

Devereaux sighed. "Don't look at me. Lieutenant Flynn ordered him placed in solitary confinement after Baldwin called him a seagoing sissy who sat down to piss."

Longarm smiled thinly at the picture. "I'll have him in leg irons if he talks that way to me on the way back to Colorado. In the meanwhile, the man's been dangerously sick and I want him at least on a cot with some solid grub in him. I'm going to have to borrow a government mount off you, which I'll naturally sign for, and it's my understanding I'll find my own Winchester, saddle, and possibles out here, where Doc Richards had 'em brought from town."

Devereaux looked unhappy. "I'm afraid we can't let you into the quarters set aside for Miss Richards before she comes back from that fever ward she's set up in town. She usually has supper out here in the officers' mess just after retreat."

Longarm nodded. "I want her to look at both Gilbert and our prisoner before I carry either into town in any case. So let's get back to getting Baldwin out of that solitary cell and wrapping him around some solid rations!"

Devereaux almost pleaded, "I can't! Lieutenant Flynn left me here to see his standing orders were carried out, not to countermand them in his absence! He'd have me before the mast for mutiny! You have to understand that Lieutenant Flynn runs a taut ship here!"

The collections of whitewashed buildings in a glorified sandbox wasn't Longarm's notion of any ship, but he saw the position the kid was in. So he asked when the ferocious Lieutenant Flynn was expected back, and when Devereaux said likely by sundown, Longarm said, "Reckon Baldwin and my old McClellan can last that long without me. I'd like to see Deputy Gilbert now."

The lieutenant rang that bell on the desk some more, and that orderly came in looking taut as ever. Devereaux told the enlisted man to show their guest to the sick bay. So it only took a few minutes, and then Longarm was alone with the pale but cheerful enough Rod Gilbert from his own outfit.

Gilbert was barely out of his teens, but according to Billy Vail, a high school graduate as well as a good shot. The department had sure gotten fancy since President Hayes had started cleaning up the federal establishment old Free and Easy Grant had left all covered with cigar ash, informal hiring practices, and graft.

Longarm sat on the steel sprung cot next to Gilbert's, noting the two of them seemed to have the eight-cot sick bay all to themselves. So as soon as he asked Gilbert how he felt he said, "They told me at least a few old boys out here came down with the same mysterious fever, Rod. So what are you doing out here alone?"

Gilbert said, "That lady sawbones, Miss Norma, wanted to carry me in to her fever ward with the rest of 'em. I said I had to stay out here and guard our prisoner. So she allowed it might be all right, seeing she's been eating and sleeping out this way."

Longarm found himself fighting back a yawn as he growled, "You ain't been guarding Baldwin worth shit if you've let 'em put a sick man on piss and punk just for sassing a fool officer! Did you know about that by the way?"

Gilbert nodded soberly. "I told 'em they had no right to punish a civilian outlaw for busting their Coast Guard rules. But they said I'd placed Baldwin under Coast Guard discipline when I asked 'em to hold him in their brig for me, and damn it, I don't know *where* they've hid my boots and side arm!"

Longarm yawned wider and said, "I want Doc Richards to look at you before the three of us shoot our way out of here. Lord, I don't know why I feel so sleepy this afternoon. When you say *they*, are you jawing about they in general, or

113

that Lieutenant Flynn they all seem so scared of for some reason?"

Gilbert said, "They got plenty of reason to be scared of Flynn. He don't yell like Billy Vail. One strike and you're out with that old boy. He's been polite enough to me, I got to say, but they do say he goes by the book and you'd best pay heed to every comma if you want to keep wearing your rating around here. They say he sends 'em to the brig if they forget to cross a T or dot an I."

Longarm let that go for the moment. In his own army days he'd had less trouble with officers who went by the book, as long as they *always* went by the book, than those assholes who cracked jokes with you one minute and expected you to fetch and carry for 'em the next. He repeated his question about the need for a Coast Guard brig to begin with, and Gilbert said, "Baldwin's crazy-mean and to tell the truth, I didn't think much of either the town lockup or the town law when I first arrived. They said Baldwin was sick. He looked more like a mad dog to me, and I got the feeling they were scared of him. I know I was scared of the half-ass cell they had him in. Brick wall bewixt him and the alley out back, for Christ's sake!"

Longarm said, "I noticed. Old Constable Purvis didn't seem too scared of anybody, albeit now that you mention it, it's sort of unusual for an arresting officer to be so disinterested in a prisoner. I know we had more exciting things to talk about, but looking back, it should have struck me odd that he never bragged at all about him or his boys catching an owlhoot rider on the run!"

Gilbert said, "I can answer that one. They never caught him. They bragged they had in that wire to Billy Vail. But if the truth be known, Clay Baldwin was in town over a month, drinking and whoring in plain view under his own given name. Nobody in town seemed to give a shit till I reckon old Clay run low on money and took to acting even worse."

As Longarm got out a couple of cheroots and his new Mexican matches, Gilbert explained. "It wasn't in that wire to us, but what they say really happened was that old Clay tried to sell some stolen stock to that meat-packing outfit in town. Reckon he figured a side of beef was a side of beef to anyone out to make a profit on it. But he figured wrong. Pryce & Doyle naturally have to be on good terms with the few big cattle spreads in these parts. So they naturally frowned upon Baldwin's business methods when they recognized those local brands on stock he said he'd just trailed down from San Antone!"

Longarm laughed as he lit both their smokes, saying, "I get the picture. I hear Pryce & Doyle use clean water in their ice machine as well. So they turned Baldwin in and . . . hold on, he trailed even a small herd of stolen cows any distance at all *alone*?"

Gilbert shook his head. "He won't tell us nothing. He's a total hardcase professional who don't give an inch. But I agree it's tough to cut and herd cows all alone. Why did you think I was so worried about that thin-walled lockup in town?"

Gilbert enjoyed a drag of smoke, let it out, and went on. "They say an indefinite number of riders stayed off to the south in a lot with the herd after dark, whilst Baldwin went into the meat packer's office to settle on a price. His gang just lit out when Baldwin never came back. He never came back because an elderly gent Baldwin took for a sissy bookkeeper threw down on him with a Walker Colt and sent an office boy to fetch Constable Purvis. The braver civilian, who was really Mister Doyle in the flesh, asked Purvis to posse up and ride after the others. But Purvis never did."

Longarm blew a thoughtful smoke ring and said, "He didn't seem so anxious to posse up after a kid got shot in the head in town this morning, come to study on it. I took it at the time as common sense. Maybe it was. But I follow your drift about Baldwin being a tad more secure out here."

He yawned again, snubbed out his barely smoked cheroot, and said, "I ain't sure solitary confinement makes him tougher for his pals to bust out, if that's who's been shooting at me lately. I know bread and water ain't what Doc Richards would prescribe for a recovering fever victim, if he's recovered worth shit. Meanwhile, as the song says, farther along we'll know

115

more about it. If I gave you my gun do you reckon you could guard me from assassination whilst I caught at least an hour's sleep?"

Gilbert nodded, but as Longarm stood to remove his hat and gun rig told him, "You can catch three or four, if you like. They don't serve supper around here before they blow horns and lower the flag around sundown. Miss Norma ain't never got back any earlier."

He might have said more. But Longarm closed his eyes before he'd finished flopping atop the covers of the empty cot, and the next thing he knew it seemed old Ruby had forgiven him after all. So he hauled her down atop him and kissed her good before he noticed she had a far bigger left tit and had pulled back mighty quickly while somewhere in the gloom young Gilbert seemed to be laughing like hell.

Then Longarm got his bearings, smiled sheepishly up at the red-faced Norma Richards, and said, "Sorry, ma'am. I thought you were somebody else."

Norma was flustered. "That seems obvious! I was only bending over to feel your brow. Your Deputy Gilbert here seems well enough to laugh like a hyena, if not fit to lead a charge uphill. I just came from the brig. But they wouldn't let me in to check on Mister Baldwin. They say he's to stay locked up alone until he learns better manners. Can they do that to even a rude civilian, Custis?"

Longarm swung his boots to the floor and held out his hand to Gilbert for his gun rig as he growled, "No. But it may take some convincing. They wouldn't let me at the Winchester you stored away for me out here either. Do you reckon I could have it now?"

Gilbert chortled, "Hot damn! Are we going to bust him out at gunpoint, pard?"

Longarm said, "Nope. I want you to stay here. Miss Norma and me are only going to feed him and take his temperature if the Coast Guard knows what's good for it."

He strapped on his gun, put on his hat, and told Norma he was ready whenever she was.

The Junoesque bacteriologist led the way, but told him she hoped he wasn't serious about armed conflict with the U.S. Coast Guard, as they strode along the veranda of the long building. He said it wasn't for him to say. It was up to them whether they wanted to let him at his own confounded federal prisoner or not.

They got to the last door down, and Norma unlocked it with a key from an apron pocket. It was dark inside with the sun way down in the western sky. But there was enough tiger-stripe light coming in through the jalousie shutters for him to make out his McClellan at the foot of the bedstead where she'd draped it over the rail. The walnut stock of his Winchester '73 saddle gun stood somewhat higher. So he hauled it from its boot and told her, "You'd best wait here a few minutes. If you don't hear shooting within ten, come on over to the brig. You'll know they let me in without a war."

She got between him and the door, pleading, "Please don't fight them, Custis. That horrid outlaw just isn't worth it. I'd tell you what he said to me the last time I tried to examine him, but you do seem mad enough already!"

He told her politely but firmly, "I ain't looking for no fight. I already knew Clay Baldwin was a worthless skunk. They sent me to bring him and young Gilbert back. They never said they wanted either of 'em dead. So stand aside and give me ten, like I said, if you don't want me grabbing you by that swell tit again."

It worked. She crawfished out of his way, blushing like a rose as she told him he was horrid. So he just strode on out, levering a round in the chamber of his Winchester as he crossed the parade with the weapon held at port.

They must have expected something like that at the guard post to the north. A chief petty officer and eight guardsmen wearing leggings, S.P. armbands, and Spencer repeaters seemed to be lined up between him and his intended goal.

Longarm stopped at easy pistol range to proclaim, "I'd be U.S. Deputy Marshal Custis Long, and I understand you're holding my own sweet federal prisoner in that brig behind you."

The C.P.O., who stood almost as tall and twice as wide as Longarm, replied in a politely firm tone, "We are, and that's where he's to remain until Lieutenant Flynn says different."

Longarm replied, just as firmly if not as politely, "I don't aim to take him off with me without your C.O.'s official release in writing. I only want to make sure he leaves here alive, and I understand you as much as told his attending physician to go jump in the lagoon."

The burly Coast Guard noncom chuckled wistfully and replied, "I'd be proud to go swimming with a gal built so swell. But that ain't what we suggested. We only told her the lieutenant told us the prisoner's to have one jar of water and two slices of white bread per diem, and no visitors until further notice."

Longarm said, "Damn it. Nobody wants to visit with the son of a bitch. I want to question him and Doc Richards wants to take his damn temperature!"

The C.P.O. nodded. "She already told us. We ain't trying to be mean to nobody, Deputy. It's just that we got orders and, well, orders are orders, see?"

Longarm said, "I got my orders too. So would you kindly order your men out of my way and unlock the damned door before somebody gets hurt?"

The C.P.O. laughed incredulously. "We heard they were sending a famous gunfighter of the civilian persuasion, Longarm. Do you really think you can get by my pistol and eight rifles with one saddle gun?"

Longarm shrugged modestly and said, "I got this six-gun at my side as well, and this Winchester fires fifteen times before I have to reload it. So make your point."

It got sort of quiet as the sun sank lower and a color guard came marching out across the parade behind Longarm's back. Then a distant female voice called out, "Custis! Stop that! That steam cutter just tied up out at the end of the pier and Lieutenant Flynn will be ashore any minute!"

Longarm and the burly N.C.O. stared silently at one another for a time. Then the Coast Guardsman said, "We ain't backing down. But this does seem a dumb time to settle it the noisy way."

Longarm replied, "Great minds seem to run in the same channels. So I reckon we'll never know who'd have won, unless your lieutenant is a really dedicated asshole."

To which the C.P.O. replied with a surprisingly boyish laugh, "Oh, I know who'd have won, and be it recorded it was your idea, not mine, to call Lieutenant Flynn an asshole."

Some of the others were grinning in the sunset's red rays as behind him they started to lower the flag. So Longarm turned about on one heel to remove his hat and stand at attention with the cocked Winchester down to one side, sincerely hoping he might not have to gun any of those nice kids.

Chapter 11

Longarm had been braced for a seagoing version of a pompous army officer he'd knocked down one time. But Lieutenant Flynn, who'd have been a captain in the army, turned out to be a sandy-haired and politely poker-faced cuss with eyes the same shade of gray as two oysters on the half shell going stale.

When Norma Richards brought him over, Flynn said it was jake with him if they wanted to listen to Clay Baldwin cuss. As that C.P.O. opened up, the lieutenant said he'd have the mess attendants save his civilian guests some supper, and turned away to go eat his own.

Longarm forgave the Coast Guard a lot when he finally got in to Baldwin's solitary cell with Norma and a lamp. Clay Baldwin didn't look like an owlhoot rider wanted for murder and grand larceny. He looked like some actor made up for the part of the village idiot in his ill-fitting duds and half-sprouted beard. As they entered, Baldwin leered at Norma and asked her, "Been getting any pronging of late, Chubby? If you ain't, I got eight inches I'd just love to have you skin for me with your tight little twat!"

Longarm snapped, "Knock it off, Baldwin. I ain't gonna say that twice."

Baldwin grinned lewdly. "Aw, have I insulted your own play-pretty, Uncle Sam? Don't worry. I ain't greedy. You can have my sloppy seconds after I show her what a real man has to offer."

And then he was flat on his ass in a far corner with a split lip as Longarm rubbed his knuckles thoughtfully and muttered, "Next time you get kicked. Guess where."

So Baldwin mentioned his balls in front of a lady, and howled like a kicked pup when Longarm kicked him there as promised.

Norma gasped, "For heaven's sake, can't you see he's crazy? Don't mistreat him further on my account. You should hear what some men call me when they're delirious with fever back in town!"

Longarm said, "This one ain't feverish. He's what we call a jail house lawyer. Someboy's misled him about what we can or can't do to a federal prisoner. Are you listening to me, you poor misled or just plain stupid rascal?"

Holding himself by the balls with both legs drawn up as he lay on one side on the concrete, Baldwin whimpered, "Damn it, Longarm, you ain't allowed to torture me. It says so in the Constitution!"

Longarm smiled down at him and replied, not unkindly, "Try sassing Judge Dickerson of the Denver District Court, once I get you back to him, if you'd like to see some cruel and unusual punishment. Are you ready to act like a grown man now, or would you like me to hold you down while the doc here gives you an enema for your own good?"

Norma blushed like hell, but laughed and declared, "I think that's a grand idea, Custis. Anyone can see this wayward youth is full of shit!"

So Clay Baldwin allowed he'd as soon behave more properly, and never said anything dirty as Norma took his pulse and temperature, hunkered down beside him in a way that surely made her white skirt tight across her ample but shapely behind.

Longarm waited until Norma took the thermometer out and said he didn't seem to be running a fever now, before he told the mean-eyed cuss, "I'll see you get a decent supper tonight. You'll eat the same as Gilbert and me on the way back to Denver. Whether you ride all the way in leg irons and cuffs or just cuffs is up to you. For as I hope you understand by now,

I treat a prisoner no better or no worse than he asks me to."

Baldwin said sullenly he'd only been funning and didn't want to stand trial back in Colorado all busted up. So Longarm nodded and said, "*Bueno*. Neither you nor Deputy Gilbert will be called upon to do much more than sit as we work our way home by boat and train. So let's hope Gilbert's as frisky as you come morning, and we might be on our way."

When Baldwin didn't argue, Longarm added, "One more thing, though. I've been having repeated problems with some pals of yours, Clay. Hamp Godwynn and Squint Reynolds are both dead."

Baldwin stared thoughtfully up at Longarm, shrugged, and asked, "Am I supposed to cry? Never heard of either of 'em. You say you gunned 'em?"

"Only Reynolds," Longarm modestly replied. "A Ranger got Godwynn up to Corpus Christi. I don't care how you feel about anyone out there in the dark. My point is that should anyone make any try at taking you away from Gilbert and me on the way out of here, you have my word you'll be among the first to die. Doc Richards here can assure you a really determined cuss can get off more than one good shot with a bullet in his heart. Ain't that right, Doc?"

Norma swallowed and declared, "Some people can remain conscious for as long as four minutes after heart failure. Don't hold me to how rational anyone might feel full of bullets!"

Longarm smiled grimly and said, "There you go, Clay. A bright boy like you ought to see the odds are better in court than in the company of a mighty unrational but highly annoyed cuss holding a gun on you!"

Baldwin wiped his bloody lip with the back of one sleeve as he insisted, "I don't know what you're jawing about. I told the boys I might have herded some stock out for parts unknown if I didn't come back with some money *poco tiempo*. You know I got double-crossed and turned over to the law. I don't know which way the others rode. We planned to split up with just such a conversation as this one in mind. I couldn't find a one of 'em now if I rode out after 'em myself. But I will say I'd be surprised to find any of 'em anywheres near Escondrijo now!"

Longarm said, "I might take your word on that if you could explain what you meant by a double cross. Are you saying you had reason to feel Pryce & Doyle might be in the market for stolen beef?"

Baldwin snorted, "Why, no, I always sell stolen property where I suspect they might call the law on me! Of course I was told that meat-packing outfit sent cold-storage meat to market with neither hides nor brands in evidence! But when I sashayed in to talk money with that prissy Mister Doyle . . . Hell, Longarm, you know the rest of my sad story."

Longarm said, "No, I don't. You never said who told you Pryce & Doyle bought stolen beef on the hoof. Would you care to illuminate me on that?"

Baldwin hesitated and then said, "Well, lots of greasers are called . . . Chino. So I reckon it won't hurt to admit it was one of the boys I met here in Texas, the lying son of a never mind."

Longarm cocked a brow and demanded, "Chino, or might it have been *Gordo*? I've a good reason to ask."

But Baldwin insisted he'd heard Pryce & Doyle peddled stolen beef from another drifter called Chino, and he was right about that being a common enough Mex nickname. So Longarm turned to Norma and suggested they go see about some supper. But she insisted on hauling out some gauze and hunkering down by the prisoner again, observing that his lip should have stopped bleeding by this time if it meant to without any help. So Baldwin allowed, and Longarm agreed, she wasn't such a bad old gal after all.

She was curious as well, asking question after question as they supped together alone in the wardroom after she'd paid another call on young Gilbert and declared him weak but likely on his way to recovery.

As they supped on officer's fare, in this case steak and mashed potatoes with cabbage, Longarm answered her questions until he got tired of talking in circles. "Sure he was lying,

Miss Norma. The man's dishonest by definition. Hardly anyone else knew I was on my way down here, even before that storm blew the telegraph lines down. The gunslicks I've nailed down as dead facts seem cut from the same outlaw cloth as Baldwin. There must have been more than two in his gang if they cut out enough stolen beef to matter. So that'd account for some leftover and even more cowardly sniping."

She poured some canned cream in her coffee, asking if he'd like some before she mentioned that Mexican angle again.

He said, "No, thanks. I like mine black, and I mean to question a Mex called Gordo before our boat leaves, when and if we can book our passage out. It works more than one way. A man running a shop next door to a meat packer might know better than most whether they were crooks or not. But why would anyone tell saddle tramps they could sell beef on the hoof there if he knew they couldn't?"

She suggested, "What if he wanted to see them arrested?"

Longarm replied, "I just said that. Only Gordo would know for certain, if he had anything at all to do with it. There's nothing I can do about that tonight. How are we coming with your mysterious plague in town, Miss Norma?"

She sighed and said, "I feel like the Red Queen in *Alice in Wonderland*, running fast as I can to stay in one place. You were awfully sweet to put me to bed like that this morning, by the way. I felt ever so much better after just a few hours of rest and it's just as well. That naughty Ruby seems to have quit on us for reasons of her own, while that Mexican girl, Consuela, seems to be turning into a great little nurse. She's been a godsend with our Spanish-speaking victims, and we seem to be getting more of them now."

The mess attendant they'd sent to the brig with Baldwin's pork and beans came back to ask if they were ready for dessert. As soon as he went into the kitchen, Longarm said, "I've been studying on that fever going round. It reminds me of an ague they were having down Mexico way when I was tracking another owlhoot rider sort of unofficially. It was up on the central mesa in late fall. They were holding that festival they call the Day of the Dead as I recall. Nobody I was interested in at the time came down with anything. It was just something you heard folks talking about as they ran all over town acting spooky in skull masks, eating candy skulls and such. They seemed to feel it was unusual to have chills and fever going around at such a time and place."

She sipped her weaker coffee thoughtfully, then mused, "Late autumn in such high, dry country doesn't go too well with the usual outbreaks of ague or malaria. You're certain the victims suffered alternate bouts of high fever and night sweats, followed by aches, pains, shivering, and feelings of utter misery?"

He nodded. "That's about the size of it. Hold it, I think they called it something like malted fever. Like I said, I had other things on my mind at the time."

Norma frowned down at her empty plate. "Malta or Mediterranean fever won't work, I'm afraid. It's true the symptoms are much the same. But you were so right about it being confined to Old Mexico."

He asked, "Is there any law saying a sick Mex suffering this Malta ague couldn't jump the border some dark and windy night to spread it up our way like the pox?"

She sighed. "There is. We've yet to isolate the exact microbe causing Malta fever, but we know it's not transmitted from one human being to another. It's a livestock plague, like hoof-and-mouth. It's endemic to Latin America, like hoof-and-mouth, and so it can stay there the same way. You know no Mexican stock is allowed north of the border unless it's been inspected a lot. The repeated inspections make it hardly worth the effort of trying to compete with beef raised on this side of the border, Custis."

He tried some black coffee. It was good. He said, "I could tell you a tale of cows crossing borders along an outlaw route called the Laredo Loop. But let's stick to real puzzles. How could a human come down with a cow ague if humans can't pass it on to one another?"

She smiled across the table at him. "From cows, of course. We're not sure how cows, goats, hogs, and other cloven-hoofed creatures pass Malta fever back and forth. But they do, at least in Mexico and the Mediterranean basin it originated in. Infected stock doesn't seem to suffer quite as much from it, which doubtless keeps it spreading throughout Latin America from some unknown port of entry. Humans somehow catch it from infected stock, and either die or slowly recover from an intermittent fever a lot like the one we've been having up this way. But it can't be Malta fever, Custis!"

He asked, "Why can't it? Because you mean to stamp your pretty foot and say so three times?"

She smiled wearily. "I see *you* read *Alice in Wonderland* too. I'll have to read up on Malta fever. At least it's possible, if you can show me someone running infected stock all the way up from Old Mexico. Cows infected with Malta fever don't run so well, and we're at least a hundred miles from the nearest crossing, right?"

Longarm nodded. "About a week's drive, not counting at least some driving *to* the border from further south. How do you go about catching the fever from some infected cow, Miss Norma?"

She said nobody knew, then gasped, "My God. Clay Baldwin did come down with *some* fever, after he drove some purloined stock into Escondrijo, just before the town's fever broke out!"

Longarm said, "I noticed. But everybody keeps telling us Baldwin and his boys stole the stock from somewhere closer. How are you at cross-country riding, and can you tell when a critter instead of a human being is coming down with any sort of ague?"

She replied, "I guess I ride all right. I'm not sure how you can ask a cow how it feels. I might be able to diagnose a really sick one, though. What's the plan?"

He finished his coffee. "I got to arrange steamer passage out with the telegraph wires still dead. So I'd best ride back to town early, leaving Gilbert and Baldwin out here for the time being. So seeing I got to ride anyways, I figured I'd get an early start and get there a tad later, after swinging wide across the higher cow country just to the west. I want to ask about the brands that meat packer spotted on Baldwin's stolen herd. If you'd care to tag along, you might want to ask how many cows have been feeling poorly in the last few weeks or months."

She grinned like a kid who'd been invited along to swipe apples. "I have the pony and sidesaddle I hired in the stable beyond the brig. When do we start?"

He said, "Crack of dawn. Texas rancheros either shoot at you or insist on feeding you something when you come visiting after sunrise. Show up at this hour and they're more likely to just shoot."

She rose from the table, saying, "If we aim to ride out before breakfast, we'd better turn in early. The lift I got from that nap in town is already wearing off."

He got to his own feet and they went outside. He naturally had to escort a lady across the parade ground in the gathering dusk. So Norma just took his arm without comment, and he had no call to discuss his other plans for the evening with her.

He had to ask the O.D. or somebody where they wanted him to turn in. If push came to shove, he figured he could flop in that empty cot next to Gilbert's again. He wanted to talk some more to Gilbert as well as the officers still up in the wardroom. For while a fairly clear picture was starting to form, there were still some fuzzy details some damned body might have some answers to.

They got back to Norma's door at the end of the officers' quarters' veranda. He didn't expect her to invite him in, and he hadn't taken her to a paid-for supper and vaudeville show. So he figured he'd better not try to kiss her good night, no matter how tempting she was smelling in the balmy night air. So he was more than surprised when it was Norma who hauled him on inside and husked, "Don't strike a match. We don't need any lamplight, and I'd as soon not have anyone gossiping about us, Custis."

Before he could ask what there might be to gossip about she was on tiptoe against him, kissing him in a far from motherly way. So there was plenty to gossip about as soon as he'd swept

127

her up in his arms and carried her over to the bed.

But as he lowered her Junoesque form to the bedspread Longarm felt it only fair to murmur, "You did hear me say I'm fixing to pay three passages south on the next coastal steamer, didn't you?"

She murmured back, "I did, and I'll be headed the other way as soon as they repair the telegraph and I can wire for a real medical team to fight that plague. Did you think I'd be this bold with any man if I thought we had time for the usual flowers, books, and candy?"

So seeing she seemed to share some of his own ideas on grabbing life's few brass rings while the merry-go-round was still going, he just helped her out of her white linens, shucked his own duds, and took her up on her fine offer.

She hissed in mingled anxiety and pleasure as he spread her big thighs and entered her tighter-than-usual but unusually hairy ring-dang-do. The nice thing about gals with big firm butts was that you didn't need to shove a pillow under them to ride just right in their love saddle. She seemed to think they fit together just right too. She commenced to move under him with a skill that belied her girlish remarks about never having met a man so big before. He felt no call to swear she was his first and only. So he just got an elbow under each of her plump knees and proceeded to pound her good as she moaned, "Oh, Jesus! Yes! But I'm not going to fall in love again! I'm not! I'm not! I'm just going to fuck like a rabbit till I can't fuck you anymore, you lovely fucking machine!"

But that wasn't what they were doing a half hour later, according to the orderly who reported in to Lieutenant Flynn, hit a brace, and barely managed not to grin as he said, "Begging the lieutenant's pardon, that civilian lawman you sent me to escort to his guest quarters doesn't seem to need any . . . of his own."

Flynn stared up from his desk thoughtfully and coldly replied, "Don't beat around the busy with me, Yeoman. Whose quarters did you find him in, if not the ones I just assigned him? There's only one woman on this post and . . . are you sure?"

The orderly said, "Ay, ay, sir. They couldn't see me as I listened through her jalousie slats to make sure. I didn't know she had company, of course, before I heard them in passing as I was searching for that deputy as the lieutenant ordered."

Flynn smiled slightly, a rare sight in the yeoman's experience, and asked, "You're certain she hadn't just invited him in for, say, a nightcap, Yeoman?"

His informant said simply, "Begging the lieutenant's pardon, it sounded like she was sucking him off. Would the lieutenant like me to call out the guard now?"

Flynn shook his sandy head without hesitation and purred, "Belay that. They're both civilians, albeit both federal employees. So why don't we give them all the rope they want, and report them to their own superiors as soon as those damned wires are back up!"

Chapter 12

So a good time was had by all, and Norma said it was a good thing she was riding sidesaddle as they rode out at the crack of dawn after hardly any sleep. She'd changed into a more practical riding habit of tan whipcord from her Saratoga trunk, although she said she hoped to have a fresh white uniform from the laundry in town on tap as soon as they got her back to her fever ward.

Longarm was right about the country rising drier on the far side of that inland trail he'd followed down from Corpus Christi. He was right about them being forced to have coffee and cake, at least, at the half-dozen spreads they managed to visit along the way. But all the stock they passed seemed fit enough in the bright morning light.

Then, just as Longarm was about convinced the lying Baldwin must have trailed sick stock up out of Old Mexico, they met two rancheros in a row who said they'd had their own branded stock returned to them by Constable Purvis after that surprisingly honest Mister Doyle had thrown down on that cow thief.

Longarm let it got the first time, but asked the second stockman with the same story why he'd been so surprised to hear Pryce & Doyle were honest meat packers.

He was told, "Oh, nobody never said they was outright crooks. But few of us like to do business with such hard bargainers. We ain't no ignorant greasers raising cows for hides and tallow. We read the market quotations in the newspapers the same as everyone else, and it's no secret the price of beef is up, way up, this year."

Longarm nodded and said, "Pryce & Doyle don't want to pay the going rates?"

To which the Texican replied with a scowl, "They ain't willing to pay last year's rates. They seem to feel they got a monopoly here as the only meat packers within miles. But I've been driving my own beef up to Corpus Christi on the hoof. It may be a bother, and I may have had to hire some extra hands, but fair is fair and I'd as soon break even selling beef in Corpus Christi than get slickered by damn Yankees rich enough to make their own damned ice!"

They thanked the irate stockman for the information and rode on. They crossed that same tidal creek, and Longarm showed her where Consuela's dad had been attacked by that gator. Norma said she doubted reptiles caught Malta fever, and that even if they did, it hadn't ought to make them go mad like dogs with hydrophobia.

As they got into town they parted friendly, or at least as friendly as Victorian folks felt proper in public. She made him promise to drop by her fever ward before he left town again, whether he found out anything more about the plague or not.

Longarm was more worried about lying cow thieves who might or might not have backshooting pals still out there. So while he still hoped to tie the gang into any infected stock from Old Mexico, he headed back to that chandlery on the waterfront to mostly ask old Gordo if anyone ever called him Chino.

This time the reception was friendlier. The fat chandler hauled Longarm into the back, and sat him at a kitchen table to pour him some *pulque* and yell at his womenfolk for some grub for their guest.

When Longarm said he'd been eating all morning, Gordo insisted he have something anyway, explaining, "A messenger from Corpus Christi got through to us a few minutes after you had left, El Brazo Largo. I hope you won't tell La Bruja we were rude to you on purpose!"

Longarm smiled and replied, "If you don't make me eat no more. Should anyone ever ask, my only honest answer would have to be that it takes a smart man to play convincingly dumb."

He sipped some *pulque*—another acquired taste some compared to alcoholic snot, although it was mostly fermented agave—and just said right out he was looking for a Mex cow thief called Chino who'd been riding with the Anglo outlaw caught next door a short spell back.

Gordo answered simply, "We heard about it. They had the stolen stock in the vacant lot down on the other side of us. I did not wish for to get any of us into it. So we stayed inside during most of the excitement. But I don't think anybody riding with the one they caught was of La Raza. Chino can mean Chinaman as well as a Mexican with a moon face and *muy indio* eyes, no?"

Longarm finished off as much of his *pulque* as he meant to, and got back to his feet. "A regular Chinaman riding the owlhoot trail sounds even wilder than a Mex, no offense. Maybe I can get some answers next door, at that meat-packing plant Baldwin got his fool self arrested in. Is it all right with you if I leave my mount out front for now?"

Gordo grinned and said, "No. When you wish for to ride again you will find El Brazo Largo's *caballo* out back, watered and fed fresh corn I save for such honored guests!"

So they shook on it and Longarm went back outside. The sun was almost directly overhead now, and some drunk was already holding up the corner of the meat-packing plant with his back, wrapped in a red serape with his big straw sombrero down over his face to keep the sun out of his eyes.

Longarm had to explore some before he found a sheet-metal-covered door that wasn't locked on the inside. The one he found had a sign that said, "Office." So he knocked, and when nobody answered, went on inside. He found himself at the foot of a long wooden stairway. As he mounted it he saw a few chinks in the vertical planking to his left, the wall to his right being solid brick. When he paused to peer through a knothole, he saw a cavernous space that reminded him of that cold-storage hold aboard the northbound steamer. The same brine pipes, frosted with ice, ran along the far brick wall. At least a hundred sides of beef hung down there on hooks you could roll along the overhead network of single rails. Longarm was more interested in such industrial details than some, but he wasn't there to study meat packing, so he went on up to the second floor and knocked on a frosted glass door. A male voice invited him in, calling out, "It's open."

The older but still spry-looking gent in his late forties regarding him from behind a desk like Billy Vail's was sitting in his shirt and vest with his expensive frock coat and pearl-gray hat hung up near the window on the far side of him. When Longarm introduced himself, the man identified himself as Mister Doyle of Pryçe & Doyle, poured them both some real bourbon, and asked how he might be of service to the federal government.

Doyle's bourbon was good and his manners were polite, but Longarm got the feeling he was wasting time. Doyle told the same tale to Longarm as he had to everyone else. He'd only seen Clay Baldwin when the rough-hewn cuss had surprised the hell out if him with an offer of stolen beef—173 cows, as close as Doyle could recall the tally. He said the local law had read the brands and cut up the herd the outlaws had left behind in a salt marsh on their way to parts unknown. He suggested Longarm check the exact tally with Constable Purvis. But he was sure none of the cows recovered had worn those fancier brands Mexican stockmen went in for, and allowed he'd never heard of anyone, Anglo or Mexican, called Chino.

Longarm agreed Clay Baldwin had been known to fib about a lot, and then said, "Let's talk about sick cows, whether stolen or bought fair and square. You'd have noticed if any of the cows you slaughtered and butchered here were sweating like hell, shivering even harder, and so forth, right?"

Doyle pursed his lips. "It should have been reported to me,

of course. Naturally I don't do any butchering myself these days."

But when Longarm asked if he might talk to the hands who did, the meat packer told him, "You'll have to come back tomorrow, when my senior partner and head butcher get back. They're on a buying trip further west, hoping to make up our next shipment at the right price."

Longarm smiled thinly and said, "I was told you gents drove a hard bargain, no offense. Stockmen around her seems to feel they'd as soon drive their beef on up the coast. Where do you reckon Clay Baldwin or his mysterious pal Chino got the notion you'd be in the market for even cheaper beef?"

Doyle looked less friendly as he primly replied, "I'm not sure I like your tone, Deputy Long! Isn't it mighty obvious that we'd have simply *bought* that beef from Baldwin if that was our game? I'll have you know I threw down on him and turned him over to the law after he offered that stock at five dollars a head C.O.D. after dark!"

Longarm nodded soberly. "That's a bargain in beef on the hoof or off, and once you'd run 'em inside downstairs, you'd have skinned 'em out of their branded hides before anyone was any the wiser. I ain't the only one who's allowed you acted honest as well as brave when those crooks approached you, Mister Doyle. It's going to take us some time to carry Baldwin back to Colorado, give him as fair a trial as he deserves, and stretch his neck as far as it can go. So he'll likely fill in some details for us between now and then. I've seen condemned crooks turn in kin for an extra slice of pie with their last meal."

He put down his shot glass and turned toward the door, saying he'd be back, maybe the next day, to talk with Doyle's senior partner and head butcher.

Doyle rose to follow him out on the landing, demanding, "Why? I just told you all that any of us know about the matter."

Longarm nodded. "I'm sure you have, no offense. But this aint the first meat-packing plant I've ever visited, and I'm sort of puzzled about just a few points somebody who gets his hands dirtier might be able to clear up."

He went down the long stairway as Doyle went back in his office. Then he headed back to the chandlery, noting that same sleepy cuss was still propped against the bricks. But what bothered him about the stranger taking an early siesta didn't sink in all the way before he heard a distant window open and somebody he could't see tossed a bottle, or glass, out to bust and tinkle on the cobbles.

Then Longarm had his gun out, covering the serape-wrapped figure at his feet as he snapped, *"Tenga cuidado, hombre! Soy tengo el filo, aqui."* And when that didn't work he tried, "I said I have the drop on you, asshole! I didn't think a real Mex drunk would be sporting those expensive Justin boots under a dirty blanket and straw sombrero!"

The fake Mexican tried shooting up at Longarm through the grimy red wool. He got off two rounds and one came close, but not as close as Longarm's pissed-off burst of fire aimed at point-blank range. So the treacherous rascal wearing a dapper Anglo riding outfit and .45-28 Starr wound up stretched out on the dust with that dumb hat blown away but half the red serape covering his face.

Longarm kicked it away as he reloaded, staring down bemused at the softly smiling face of a total stranger as he reloaded. The dumb bastard looked to be around fifty. Longarm had just hunkered down to go through some pockets when Gordo, from next door, came timidly over to make the sign of the cross and shyly ask, "For why did you shoot Señor Pryce just now, El Brazo Largo?"

Longarm was back on his feet and moving off as he called back, "I had to. He was fixing to backshoot me again. Tell Purvis who did it when he gets here. I'll tell him why as soon as I get back with his sneaky partner, Doyle!"

He didn't waste time chasing around inside the packing plant on foot after a sneak who'd already signaled he was to be shot on the way out. He tore around the back of Gordo's chandlery, hauled that Coast Guard pony out of his brushwood stable, and forked himself up into his army saddle to ride after the son of a bitch.

The best way to chase another cuss was to figure which way he'd likely head, not give him a greater lead while you asked others for directions. So Longarm loped across the main street and headed west along that same lane leading to the inland wagon trace. For a man on the run with the law hot on his heels would likely choose some solitude as he lathered his own brute, and the coast road ran through much more of town as well as past that Coast Guard station to the north. All bets were off if the bastard was riding south, but from what La Bruja had told Longarm the shady meat packers had at least one mighty shady confederate up in Corpus Christi, if one of the partners themselves hadn't been trying to recruit Mexicans to drygulch a dangerous Anglo.

He had a better handle now on why they'd considered him dangerous. Thanks to old Reporter Crawford of the *Denver Post*, a lot of folks knew the notorious Longarm had spent some time punching cows before going to work under Marshal Billy Vail. Yet he'd missed what they were up to, and might have never studied on a dinky meat packing operation in a dinky seaport if they'd been smart enough to leave him the hell alone. There were heaps of stockmen coming and going all around the establishment of Pryce & Doyle, yet how many had ever seen fit to wonder how you ran a slaughterhouse without any stockyards out back, or why the tallow-rendering plants, fertilizer mills, and tanneries you usually saw next to a slaughterhouse hadn't been anywhere in the whole blamed town.

He was sure he had more answers than he really did as he tore out to the west with his saddle gun cocked across his knees, eyes peeled for ambush from the cactus hedges around the small *milpas* he tore by.

Then he spotted a small familiar figure afoot ahead, and reined in as that young Mexican gal Consuela turned around in the dusty road with a puzzled look on her pretty little face.

Longarm called out, "I'm chasing that sneaky meat packer, Doyle. Might you have seen him out this way, on most any sort of transportation? I suspect he signaled his partner the jig was up and lit out when I got that partner instead."

136

Consuela stared up owl-eyed to reply, *"Pero no, señor.* I am on my way home for to search for wicked *cabras* my little brother just told me about. I told La Señorita Norma I had to go find them for Papacito before *la aligador* gets them. I do not know for why they run off into the spartina reeds like that when they are feeling bad, but they do, and I know where to search for them."

He said he felt sure she did, and started to wheel his mount around to try another direction when what she'd said sank all the way in and he said, "Hold on. You say your goats have been coming down sick, Consuela?"

She said, *"Sí,* more than half of them. *Pero* not all at once. One gets to shaking and dragging its poor hooves and then, just as it seems to feel better, another we thought was well again starts to cry and butt its head against things."

"Like those folks in town!" Longarm gasped. "Sick goats wandering into the swamps to get eaten by gators could account for a hungry gator boldly backtracking to your *milpa* in hopes of more goat meat and settling for . . . Do you folks sell a lot of goat meat in town, Consuela?"

She burst that bubble by shaking her head and declaring, *"Pero no!* Where would we get the milk for to make cheese or put in coffee if we slaughtered our milk goats for meat, *señor?"*

Longarm didn't answer. He was already headed back to town, as fast as he'd just ridden out. As he hit the main street again he saw a considerable crowd to his right, near the meat-packing plant. He swung the other way, slid his mount to a stop in front of the old icehouse, and tore inside, calling out to Norma, "Hey, Doc, I think I got it!"

The Junoesque Norma came across the cot-cluttered floor to meet him, looking innocent, in her fresh white outfit. But she smiled awfully sweet as she asked him in a puzzled tone what on earth he was talking about.

Longarm said, "You were right about it being a fever carried by livestock. But it was the nondescript Mex goats that nobody pays much attention to. No cows have caught it yet. Goats

137

don't graze on open range with Texas beef cows, in peril of their lives."

She nodded but said, "That only makes sense till you consider all the Anglos coming down with your mysterious goat fever, Custis. How many of these Anglo townsfolk, cowhands, and even Coast Guardsmen do you suspect of eating or even petting sick Mexican goats?"

Longarm insisted, "It's the *milk*. None of those spreads we passed this morning kept one dairy cow on hand. Like everyone else down this way they buy the little fresh milk and cream they fancy off the local smallholders, who keep goats, not cows, for milking!"

Norma Richards was smart as well as passionate. So she thought, snapped her fingers, and said, "Of course! You don't take cream in your coffee. I've been using canned condensed milk, here as well as out at that Coast Guard station, thanks to a generous mess officer who asked me not to mention it to Lieutenant Flynn."

Longarm said, "Flynn seems to strike lots of folk as a martinet. Either way, condensed milk explains why so few Coast Guardsmen came down with this fever, and how come the ones in your care seem to be getting over it naturally."

But Norma was already waving all her volunteer gals in, along with some recovering patients she'd been putting to work there. Longarm didn't hang about to hear her explain why they all had to dash through town, shouting like Paul Revere about getting rid of all the fresh milk and goat cheese on hand. He was already on his way to get back to his own chores.

As he strode for the mount he'd tethered out front, old Constable Purvis cut him off, side arm drawn, demanding, "Stand and deliver on how come you just shot a pillar of our community, Deputy Long!"

Longarm said tersely, "Had to. It was him or me. I suspect that once we pass around some photographs, we'll agree those others I took for saddle bums were business associates of the late Mister Pryce as well. They must have had a time getting their regular help to go up against me and my rep, if they got desperate enough for the senior partner to try for me personally! I got to catch the junior partner now, and see if I can get him to fill me in on some of the missing pieces of the puzzle. I'm sure I got most of it about right now."

He untethered his mount and started to mount up as the older law man pleaded, "Tell *me* what's been going on here, damn it! I can't make heads or tails of a thing that's happened. How could Pryce & Doyle have been running a crooked operation if they turned in the only crook who ever stole one cow in these parts? Nobody for miles is missing any stock, old son!"

Longarm saw there was no way an elder on foot could ride along with him as they jawed, so he patiently explained. "Nobody for miles was doing business with Pryce & Doyle. They were afraid I'd notice other missing details as well. They had nothing resembling a full-fledged meat-packing operation. No stockyards, no side rendering plants, and shit, not even a slaughtering floor inside that glorified icebox. Just as they feared, albeit I had other things on my mind at the time, all I saw on their premises was a cold-storage cargo hold of neatly butchered beef. The same as I saw aboard a coastal steamer the other night. Don't you get it yet?"

Constable Purvis ran a thumbnail through the stubble on his jaw and declared, "Makes no sense. Pryce & Doyle have been shipping their cold-storage beef out of here regular. So where's it been bred, reared, and butchered if it ain't been around here?"

Longarm swung up in the saddle, saying, "Old Mexico, most likely. That's the only place near enough to matter where they could have got prime sides of neatly trimmed beef so cheap. When I catch Doyle I mean to ask him whether he refused Baldwin's offer because he thought it might be a trap or whether you can still buy beef on the hoof at five bucks a head down Mexico way."

"But how in thunder would you get all them Mex cows this far north past the hoof-and-mouth quarantine this spring?" the older lawman wailed as Longarm headed on, having wasted enough time guessing when all he had to do was catch the son of a bitch who knew!

Chapter 13

An old Mexican leading a burro loaded with firewood told Longarm he was on the right trail now, although the gringo on the lathered roan had one hell of a lead on him. There was no way anyone out at that Coast Guard station could have heard about recent events in town. And there was nobody to wire this side of Corpus Christi. No pony could run that far in one burst, though. So it all hinged on how hard either rider could push what he was riding. The coldblood bay saddle breed Longarm had borrowed wasn't considered all that fast but might have a tad more endurance, or a few less brains, than the cow pony Doyle seemed to be riding. So Longarm could only keep heeling his bay at a steady lope and hope for the best.

The treacherous Doyle had a more jaded pony or more treacherous nature than Longarm should have expected by now. Virtue might have been its own reward, but had he never pulled off into that tangle of gumbo-limbo with old Ruby, he might not have been glancing over that way now as he tore past their recent love nest.

And he might not have seen the big white cotton ball of gunsmoke and rolled off the far side, Winchester in hand, by the time the rifle report that went with a whizzing .45–70 made it as far as he'd just been.

He hit the grassy seaward berm of the wagon trace any old way, and rolled a couple of times as that unseen but hardly unknown bushwhacker whacked at him some more with that repeating rifle. Longarm lost his hat, and his saddle and possibles lit out down the trace aboard that gun-shy government mount. It served a rider right for not borrowing one off the cavalry. But Longarm knew the bay would bolt for its own stall at the nearby Coast Guard station, and right now he had more important things to worry about than spare socks!

Since they'd laid out that wagon trace along a contour line, Lord love 'em, the soft soggy soil on his seaward side lay almost a yard lower than the roadway, and better yet, the salt grass he'd been rolling through rose well above his prone form. The son of a bitch firing from the gumbo-limbo across the way was aiming at the swaying grass tops, not at a target he couldn't really draw a tight bead on at that range.

Longarm slithered around on his belly, ignoring the repeated potshots above as well as across his ass, till he was facing the way he'd been coming instead of the way he'd been going when he hit the ground. But what made it work was rolling close to the wagon trace till he lay between the slight rise and the long grass stems about half a yard out, on untouched and hence damper ground. He still moved slow, like a rat snake sneaking into a root cellar, dragging his '73 by its long barrel for what felt like a hundred miles but was likely a hundred yards. Then he made some nearby salt grass move with the muzzle of his Winchester, and when nothing happened he figured Doyle had to be back in that blind alley Longarm had backed into with Ruby, or another like it. So he took a deep breath, gathered his long legs under his center of balance, and sprang up to dash across the wagon trace, between two cottonwoods and through the open space on the far side, till he'd made the gumbo-limbo himself and got his breath back. Then he called out laconically, "That reminded me of Cold Harbor, Doyle. I sure hope we don't have to repeat that infernal campaign, for we could both wind up getting hurt in a blindman's buff with shooting irons. Why don't you quit whilst you're ahead? You'll likely get away with blaming your dead pals for all the hanging offenses. That's if the prosecution agrees to let you turn state's evidence and tie up some loose ends for us."

Doyle fired blind through the springy saplings between them. As his ricochet wailed harmlessly off in the distance, Longarm chuckled and called back falsely, "Close. But no cigar. I don't want to have to kill you, asshole. I've about figured out what you and your pals were up to. But my boss frowns on what he calls my suppositions. You call it a supposition when you can't prove it. But you know I know a hell of a lot already. You wouldn't have tried to stop me from ever getting anywhere near your flimflam packing plant if you hadn't been worried about me taking one look and asking what in blue blazes you thought you were running there."

Doyle fired again. Longarm swore. "I got you boxed, you poor simp. I was back in those saplings just the other day and I know how tight they grow. I'm willing to ignore your repeated attempts to murder a federal agent recently, if you'd like to settle for just a few years in Leavenworth on smuggling and criminal conspiracy in exchange for a few more names, dates, and places."

Doyle didn't answer. Longarm spotted movement further up that wagon trace in a place exposed to fire from the thicket, and called out, "Get off that trail, boys! I got me an armed and stupid outlaw trapped up this way with a repeating rifle!"

As the Coast Guardsmen crabbed westward to form a more cautious file, hugging the gumbo-limbo to the north of where Doyle seemed to be, Longarm recognized Lieutenant Devereaux, leading the patrol with a Spencer of his own held at port arms. As the junior grade got within easy shouting range he called out, "That mount we loaned you just tore through the gate lathered under your empty saddle. So we doubted the distant shots we kept hearing could be a duck hunter. Who have we got pinned down here, Deputy?"

Longarm called back, "Old Doyle of Pryce & Doyle in town. Pryce tried to backshoot me earlier. So we don't have to worry about him right now. As near as I can put it together, they were running Mexican beef to the U.S. market through that hoof-and-mouth quarantine along the border this season. They were offering local stockmen insulting prices for Texas beef, partly reflecting what they were paying Mex meat packers for already butchered and trimmed sides, but mostly because they had no facilities of their own for dealing with beef on the hoof." He turned his head to shout through the gumbo-limbo saplings. "I hope you're paying attention to this, Doyle. I got you pinned with the help of the U.S. Coast Guard, organized by Secretary Alexander Hamilton of the U.S. Treasury in the first damned place to keep smugglers like you in line!"

Doyle fired his rifle back at Longarm like a mean little kid. As some of the Coast Guardsmen raised their own weapons Longarm barked, "Hold your fire! He ain't so dangerous as desperate, and I aim to take at least one of them alive!"

Devereaux repeated Longarm's command, since it sounded more official coming from him, and called out to the trapped smuggler to surrender in the name of the U.S. Revenue Service.

Doyle didn't answer. They they all heard hoofbeats, and down the road came Lieutenant Flynn himself, waving his dress saber aboard a bay thoroughbred. As Devereaux warned him off by pumping his own rifle over his own head, the sandy-haired C.O. slid his handsome mount to a stop and dismounted gracefully, if somewhat dramatically, waving that nickel-plated blade like a seagoing version of J. E. B. Stuart or George Armstrong Custer. You had to give even a pain in the ass credit for being a good rider.

Devereaux filled his C.O. in, out of easy earshot, on the north side of the trapped Doyle. Longarm knew what they'd been jawing about when Flynn called out, "All right, Mister Doyle, you have ten seconds and counting to throw out your weapon and come out with your hands up! I now make it seven and still counting!"

Longarm bawled, "Hold on! We got him boxed, Lieutenant!" Meanwhile, deeper in the gumbo-limbo, Doyle wailed something that sounded like, *"A mo abra! Fan ort! Is cruinte mi!"*

Then Flynn shouted, "Volley, fire!" and nobody paid Longarm a lick of attention as he shouted himself hoarse above the rattle of rifle fire, with each infernal Spenser firing seven times before anyone had to stop!

In the ringing silence that followed, Longarm croaked, "Asshole! How am I supposed to take 'em alive with help like that?"

Flynn said coldly, "You heard me warn him. That sounded like some ancient Irish war cry he threw back at us. Does anyone here have the Gaelic?"

Longarm snorted in disgust and said, "I wanted him to testify in English before a federal grand jury. I'm going in now. If any of you fill me full of lead, I'll never speak to you again!"

Devereaux warned, "Be careful, we were firing blind!"

Longarm eased up to that wilted sea grape he'd piled across the very same gap the day before. Now he muttered, "I noticed. There might be enough of him left to make a dying statement."

But there wasn't. Longarm had only moved in about as far as where he'd backed Ruby's shay before he spotted Doyle, further back among the supple saplings than he'd have thought possible. But Doyle had been sort of wiry as well as desperate. So there he stood, still on his feet, staring blankly as the blood still oozed from a good two dozen gunshot wounds.

Longarm propped his Winchester against two closely grown trunks and reached into the tangle, with some effort, till he had a grip on one of the dead man's sleeves. It was still a chore to wriggle Doyle out, even dead as the snows of yesteryear and limp as an old man's dick after a whole night in a whorehouse.

Devereaux joined him in the sun-dappled grotto, holding Longarm's Stetson in his free hand as he said, "One of my men just found your hat across the way. Is he dead?"

Longarm picked up his Winchester and took back his Stetson as he replied, "Yep. Didn't get much out of him as he breathed his last in a mishmash of English and that odd lingo . . . Gaelic, you say?"

Devereaux said, "Don't look at me. We were part of the Protestant gentry in the old country, to hear my grandmother go on. It could have been Gaelic. Or it could have been Greek, for all *I* know."

Longarm said, "I've known some Irish gals who burst into Gaelic when they were feeling sore at me, or vice versa. It may as well have been Greek to me, but I think Doyle's a Scotch or Irish name."

Devereaux asked, "What about Pryce, his late partner's handle?"

Longarm said, "Welsh, I think. His other pals, Godwynn and Reynolds, sound like they had plain English names to me. In the meanwhile, we ain't going to get much more than bug-bit hanging about in this baby jungle!"

Devereaux agreed, and said he'd deal with the cadaver. So Longarm stepped back out in the sunlight, where Flynn asked much the same questions and got about the same answers. While everyone but the big cheese on the bay got to walk the short distance to the nearby Coast Guard station, Longarm asked how Deputy Gilbert and their prisoner, Baldwin, might be making out.

Flynn said, "They both seem on the road to recovery. I'm not sure I see how the outlaw they sent you and Gilbert after might fit into this wild whatever that Pryce & Doyle were up to."

Longarm said, "Baldwin don't fit at all, Lieutenant. He was wanted on other charges entirely, and got his fool self arrested when he tried to sell stock he'd stolen close by to other crooks who'd picked this nice quiet stretch of coast to ship cold-storage meat from. Escondrijo's close enough to Old Mexico for a crooked outfit to pick up quarantined beef, at a considerable bargain, but far enough from the border to avoid suspicion as to where in this world they ever came by it."

Devereaux, walking on the other side of Longarm, asked how they'd ever managed to move cold-storage beef by the ton across more than a hundred miles of Texas cattle country.

Longarm said, "They couldn't have. So they never did. I figure they smuggled the forbidden Mex beef in from some

Mex port such as Matamoros. No Mex officials would have call to worry about an outward-bound cargo and even if they did, you can buy most anyone working for El Presidente Diaz cheap."

Devereaux frowned thoughtfully and said, "That sounds needlessly complicated to me! Once a vessel put safely out from Matamoros with a load of refrigerated beef, what was there to prevent it from going on up to, say, Galveston or New Orleans to unload?"

Longarm said, "You boys. The U.S. Coast Guard can't watch every tub leaving Old Mexico or even plying these coastal waters, as long as it acts natural. But how would you go about putting in to some major seaport with a valuable load and no proper bill of lading?"

From the far side, Lieutenant Flynn almost snapped, "It's all so obvious now that the scheme's been exposed, Mister Devereaux. Pryce & Doyle simply acted as a way station for their seagoing confederates. Probably putting in from the open sea through Corpus Christo Pass in one of those innocent-looking fishing luggers we only occasionally check now and again. With their own more elaborate ice plant they could afford to amass a respectable cargo, which they'd then load aboard one of those coastal steamers that had already passed through U.S. Customs down by the mouth of the Rio Grande. Delivered with proper papers up the coast as Texas beef, nobody would have been the wiser had only they had the sense to leave Deputy Long here free to carry out his own less complicated mission. What was the name of that Mexican crone who's said to smuggle contraband in from the high seas, Mister Devereaux?"

The J.G. said, "La Bruja, sir. That means The Witch in Spanish, and I must say she and her gang have been a bitch to intercept on land or sea. The Rangers say she runs small but valuable cargoes past us in a splinter fleet of shallow-draft luggers with black sails, at low tide in the dark of the moon."

Longarm didn't see how he could object that La Bruja ran guns, not sides of beef in unrefrigerated holds, unless he wanted to answer more questions about a lady than he really needed to. So he let them gas on and on about all the ways one might smuggle beef on ice in a hot, humid clime. And then they'd made it back to the Coast Guard station, where a lawman juggling a whole drawer full of knives might be able to set at least a few of them aside, for the moment.

Chapter 14

Both Doyle's roan and the bay packing Longarm's personal saddle had passed through the gate before them, to be rounded up and put away with the water they'd likely had in mind when they bolted.

Longarm found young Deputy Gilbert dressed as well as back on his feet, although still a mite green around the gills. Clay Baldwin seemed in fair shape to travel as well, having had a heap of fight knocked out of him by that long siege of off-and-on chills and fever.

But Longarm decided a few more hours' rest wouldn't hurt either after he carried Doyle's scrawny cadaver back to town to be photographed, buried, or stuffed, for all the federal government really cared. Flynn seemed to feel both crooked meat packers ought to go in the files as solved smuggling cases. But Longarm pointed out, "Texas will want to file 'em for murder for certain, and thanks to your love of noise, I ain't sure how I'd ever prove either guilty of anything else in a court of law, Lieutenant."

Flynn said stubbornly, "I did what I thought best. You said yourself he was trying to eel his way back through those springy saplings when only a small part of our volley stopped him. Didn't he say anything the federal government could use against him, Deputy Long?"

Longarm shrugged and said, "I'm still working on that. It's tough to say just what a shot-up cuss is trying to tell you when he gets to blowing bloody bubbles and a mishmash of English and Gaelic at you. Might you have anyone in your outfit who follows the drift of Ancient Irish, Lieutenant?"

Flynn thought. "Chief Tobin's people were from Galway, still considered Apache country by Queen Victoria. I could send for him, if you like."

Longarm considered, shrugged, and decided, "Maybe later. If he wasn't with us out yonder, I ain't sure I could reproduce the funny noises for him. Like I told this circus lady who swallowed swords and cussed in Gaelic, it sounds like a mishmash of Church Latin and Dutch, neither of which finds me at all fluent. Can you recall one word he yelled back when you ordered him to surrender?"

Flynn shook his head. "My people came over from Cork three generations ago. I understand my great-grandparents had been speaking English some time before they got on the boat."

The dapper Coast Guard officer seemed even smugger than usual as he added with a lofty sniff, "We Flynns arrived with shoes on. Nobody in my family was still there when the potato crop failed in '46."

Longarm allowed he'd heard a General Sullivan had led Continental troops up the Mohawk Valley during the even earlier American Revolution, and suggested they worry about old Doyle's family tree farther along, like the old hymn said.

He told Flynn and the other officers assembled in the wardroom he had other chores in town, but hoped to bring Norma Richards back that evening so she could give his deputy and their surviving prisoner a final examination. When Devereaux asked what might keep him that busy the rest of the day in town, Longarm explained, "Aside from signing a statement on two dead residents for the local law, I got to see that packing plant is sealed, with all that uncertain beef refrigerated as well as impounded. We're pretty certain now that that outbreak of Malta fever was occasioned by the milk of sick local goats. But Lord knows what all they might have smuggled in with the carcasses of Mex stock butchered and cooled down in hoof-and-mouth country!"

They agreed nobody ought to sample any such beef before somebody who knew more about such matters took a good close look at it. Flynn told Devereaux to make sure Longarm got plenty of help in wrapping the late Mr. Doyle in a tarp and loading him aboard a buckboard for his return to town.

The J.G. naturally ordered Chief Tobin to see to it. The burly C.P.O. hadn't been out there with the others when Flynn had ordered his fatal fusillade. But as they were wrapping the shot-up Irishman in waterproof canvas, Tobin observed he'd heard the poor bastard had tried to give up at the last.

When Longarm asked how the chief knew this, Tobin looked around as if to make sure no officers were listening as he confided, "Yeoman Cohen would be a Sligo man, as odd as some Yankees might be finding that. He tells us Doyle shouted something like, 'Oh, me eyebrow, hold your fire for it's finished I am!' Cohen tried to tell the others, but they were already firing. So he fired too."

Longarm said he'd noticed that. Then, rank having its privileges, the chief dragooned some guardsmen firsts to load the cadaver on the buckboard and hitch Doyle's rested roan to the wagon.

Longarm allowed he'd ride the same steady bay, seeing it was as ready to go. When Tobin asked whether he was expecting any more cross-country riding, Longarm said you just never knew.

Mounting up and taking the roan's ribbons to lead instead of drive, Longarm told his enlisted pals he'd try to get back by suppertime so they could put his borrowed pony away.

As he headed across the parade for the gate, he was headed off by young Devereaux, afoot, who called out, "The lieutenant's compliments, and if you can't manage steamer passage in town for you and your party, he said to tell you we'll be running our own night patrol aboard our own cutter, if the three of you would like a free ride to a more important port!"

Longarm told Devereaux he and his own boys might take the Coast Guard up on such a kind offer, adding, "Depends on what else I find out in town. When are you all putting out to sea this evening?"

Devereaux said, "With the evening ebb tide. About three hours after sundown tonight."

Longarm saw that gave him plenty of time to study on it. So he said he would, and headed on back to Escondrijo, having no trouble with either pony in the soggy heat of a lazy day in South Texas.

From the way folks carried on in town, you'd think they'd never had two dead men propped up on a cellar door to admire before. More than one local historian had a box camera to record the slack-jawed features of Pryce & Doyle for posterity although Constable Purvis didn't think much of Longarm's suggestion that they have the two sons of bitches stuffed. Purvis said he meant to store them in their own cold-storage plant once a few pissed-off citizens got through spitting on 'em. So while some of that went on, Longarm and the older lawman had some cold beer across the way and Longarm brought Purvis up to date on the case, such as it was.

Purvis opined the boys had likely been in with that notorious Mexican gang led by the mysterious La Bruja up the coast a ways, until Longarm pointed out, "I've personal reasons for leaving those Mex smugglers out of it. To begin with, they warned me about these other crooks in time to save my ass. They'd have never done so if they'd been in tight with a bunch of Anglo smugglers."

He sipped more beer. "After that, Pryce or Doyle going to La Bruja for help against me tells us something else. Had they had a really big bunch working with 'em, they'd have never recruited half-ass killers who got killed themselves, or had to start gunning for me so personally. With four faces photographed fairly fresh, the Rangers ought to be able to tie the ones we got so far with any associates still at large."

Purvis looked dubious. "I dunno, old son. Nobody in town's been able to identify that one you sent ashore here after you shot him on board that steamer the other night."

Longarm nodded. "That only means he wasn't from

151

Escondrijo. I just said the operation has to be spread mighty thin along a heap of thinly populated coastline. Someone is sure to recognize one or more photograph betwixt Matamoros and, say, Galveston. Right now, I'm more worried about how in blue blazes they got all that forbidden beef this far north of Matamoros."

Purvis suggested, "It's a mighty big lagoon, with many a cove and shallow-draft grass flat, Longarm. Anyone can see why they picked our particular port. We do ship honest beef out of here, albeit mostly alive, aboard cattle boats. So once the smugglers got past the revenue cutters guarding the mouth of the Rio Grande, or Corpus Christi Pass, which is even closer, they just had to unload by the dark of night when all us honest folks were in bed and then ship it right on, in broad-ass working hours, as honest Texas beef. Ain't that a bitch?"

Longarm finished his schooner. "A heap of trouble for a marginal profit too. Say the gang was small and they had plenty of cheap beef to move. They still must have had a less risky way to bring it in from Old Mexico than you just suggested. We're talking perishable produce, not diamonds or even gold bullion. They thought they had a good thing worth protecting here. I just can't see midnight runs with black-sailed luggers playing tag with steam cutters for the amount of financial reward that would go with such penny-ante bullshit. Crooks stealing shit worth less'n a dollar a pound on the retail market back East need to move it by the ton, with little or no fear of getting caught!"

Purvis pointed out, "They sure were afraid of getting caught by you, weren't they?"

Longarm grimaced. "They were, in a desperate penny-ante way. They acted more like mean pimps trying to protect a street corner. That means they didn't have local protection, which is why I feel so free to talk about 'em with you."

Purvis cocked a brow. "Why, thank you, I reckon. What if they just had that cold-storage meat brung up from Matamoros in the cold-storage holds of that coastal steamer line? They'd only need a few key henchmen with an otherwise honest outfit.

152

Who else would be peeking inside a sealed-up section of the steamer like so?"

Longarm rose back to his feet, saying, "I did, the other night. I didn't pay much attention at the time. They'd have been better off leaving me the hell alone. But dumb as I might have been, your notion falls apart as soon as you put out from, say, Matamoros with a load of quarantined beef. Getting out is no big boo. But getting into the innocent stream of coastal traffic would be. Whenever the Coast Guard stops a vessel coming in from parts unknown, they send a search party aboard."

Purvis asked, "Is there any law saying Coast Guard officers can't be paid off?"

Longarm said, "No *natural* law. Federal statutes take a mighty dim view of it. So do I. So I've naturally considered that already. It keeps boiling down to the root of all evil, the love of your average cuss for money! How much do you reckon it would take to bribe a whole Coast Guard, or even one cutter crew out of one station?"

Purvis considered and decided, "You'd sure have to sell a hell of a lot of ground round back East at T-boned prices!"

Longarm agreed that was about the size of it, and left to see how good old Norma and her plague might be making out.

Up by the converted icehouse, he found that for a soft flutterly gal who liked to be on the bottom best, the motherly but somewhat bossy Norma Richards had been making out just fine.

After kissing him smack on the mouth in front of everybody, the Junoesque doctor told him she'd wired a list of the observed symptoms all the way to the Surgeon General's office, and been assured they sure seemed to add up to Malta or what some now called undulant fever. They'd told her she'd been making sense with the moves she'd made so far, and suggested other, more drastic measures she might take to check the plague till a team from back East could get there to help her.

When she shyly asked whether he thought that meant she'd be in charge, Longarm kissed her some more and assured her, "If it don't, there ain't no justice. But when did they get the wires back up and how come nobody told me?"

She said, "I just found out myself. Western Union hasn't been advertising for more business and the backlog is still awesome. I had to buck the line by threatening them with the power of the federal government. But I'm sure you'll be able to break in the same way, citing a federal emergency."

Longarm smiled thinly and replied, "I've never admired folks who got in line ahead of me, and there's nothing I have to say that can't wait till things simmer down a mite. I'd rather talk about Rod Gilbert and our sick prisoner, Baldwin. Lieutenant Flynn's offered us a free ride out aboard his steam cutter, and I was hoping you'd be able to tell me they were fit to travel."

Norma favored him with a maternal smile and sighed. "You've no idea how tempted I am to keep the three of you here for a month of Sundays, darling. But if you're asking me in my official capacity, the course of undulant fever is pretty predictable."

She took his arm as if to lead him off to show him something as she explained. "Thanks to your inspired guess about infected goat's milk and, as it turns out, local buttermilk-fed pork, we've stopped any human beings around here from being re-infected. We're not certain how vegetarian cows pass the plague along, but it's tougher for people to pick up. They have to rub body fluids from an infected animal into an open cut, or swallow them in greater quantity. You already know how sick they get within a few days. But it's called undulant because of the way it comes and goes, with each attack both milder and farther apart."

She was leading him out a side door for some reason as she went on. "It's usually the second or third attack that those who die succumb to. It's not as much the fever itself, as the pneumonia or secondary ailments that hit a victim in his or her drained state. Young Gilbert and that dreadful Clay Baldwin have been through the whole cycle half a dozen times. So I'm sure they're out of danger, albeit either may have mighty bad days for as long as a year in the future."

Longarm said he doubted Clay Baldwin had that much future

ahead of him, and as she led him up the outside stairs of the building to the north added, "I reckon I can get them both back to Denver sitting down or stretched out aboard public transportation. Where might you be leading me, Miss Norma?"

She giggled sort of dirty and replied, "Down the Primrose Path, or at least up to the new quarters I've commandeered for myself here in town, now that I seem to be the Public Health Service. I had far less privacy as well as a longer trip back and forth at that Coast Guard station!"

She didn't say where she'd be taking her meals, now that she was quartered closer to her fever ward. Longarm didn't really care, once she'd shut the door upstairs behind them and turned with a Mona Lisa smile to confide, "Cross-ventilation too. But now that I have you in my wicked power, in broad daylight for heaven's sake, are you sure I can trust you not to laugh at your poor little piggy?"

Longarm proceeded to shuck his own duds too as he asked her when he'd ever declared her a pig. He managed not to laugh as she proceeded to pop a lot of bulging pink flesh in view, demurely suggesting, "This is the first time we've ever seen one another naked in daylight. I do try to watch my weight, dear, but it gets harder and harder as a girl gets older and . . . Oh, my God, did you really put all *that* in me the other night?"

He suggested soothingly that they see if they still fit fine together where it really counted. As he laid her back across her brass-railed bed atop the covers, she bit her baby-girl lower lip and hissed, "Be careful with that thing, Custis!"

But then, a few minutes later, being fickle as most gals about such matters, she was pounding his bare ass with the heels of her high-buttons, demanding he go deeper if he knew what was good for him.

So what with one position and another, with a quick supper shared well after sundown at the beanery across the way, Longarm barely made it back to the Coast Guard station in time to board that steam cutter as it cast off on a falling tide.

Like most of its breed, the long white-hulled cutter was

155

mostly flash boilers, powerful engines, and four-pound deck guns capable of catching up with anything its twin screws couldn't.

Chief Tobin told them Flynn and young Devereaux were too busy on the bridge to talk to anyone right now. But meanwhile, they could lock Baldwin in the ship's brig forward, and they'd try to make the two civilian lawmen comfortable in the wardroom, aft and a short length of ladder down from the bridge. Longarm had noticed before how sailors called any sort of steps "ladders," any sort of floors "decks," and so forth. Cowhands liked to confound green hands the same way.

A mess attendant brought the two deputies coffee, and said something about a smoking lamp being lit. Rod Gilbert still said he'd feel far better smoking out on deck instead of there in the greasy-smelling wardroom as the cutter began to pick up speed. For narrow-beam steamers tended to roll far more than sailboats, even across the calmer waters of a sheltered lagoon.

It was a good thing Gilbert felt that way. For they'd barely made it out to where Longarm could see the stars before he saw they weren't headed the way he'd expected.

Gilbert tagged wanly along as Longarm went on up to the bridge to demand why. What they called a bridge on a Coast Guard cutter was more like a glorified pilothouse borrowed from a riverboat. Lieutenant Flynn was posing for a statue behind the enlisted man at their big oak wheel and brass binnacle. It was Devereaux, acting as first officer, who cut them off and said they weren't allowed on the bridge while a patrol was in progress.

Longarm calmly but firmly replied, "That's what we're here to ask you about. How come we're headed south? Ain't you boys assigned to pay more heed to vessels putting in through Corpus Christi Pass to your north? There ain't no way to smuggle anything in off the open sea this side of the Rio Grande, one hell of a voyage to the south!"

Flynn turned grandly and stiffly replied, "As the one and only master of this vessel I don't have to answer to you or anyone else. But I've set a course for Matamoros because that's where you keep saying someone's been picking up quarantined beef. Didn't you also say you came all this way via the Rio Grande and up this very lagoon?"

Longarm sighed. "I did. I thought it would be obvious, even to you, I'd want to compare notes with the Rangers and others I know in Corpus Christi before we headed on back some other way!"

Flynn shrugged. "You should have asked which way we were headed before you boarded this evening. I understand the telegraph wires are back up. You ought to be able to contact all the others you want by Western Union once we put you ashore at Brownsville."

Longarm insisted, "I don't want to give any other crooks that much of a lead on me, Lieutenant. While I'm wasting a whole night aboard this cutter, patrolling miles of doubtless empty lagoon, confederates of Pryce & Doyle will be covering their crooked tracks with heaps of razzle-dazzle!"

It was Devereaux who quietly suggested, "Should the lieutenant so desire, we could put these civilians ashore at Escondrijo. I think I see the lamplight along their quay just ahead, off to starboard."

Flynn snapped, "You're not paid to think, Mister Devereaux. Until such time as they give you your own command, you'll be expected to do just as you're damned well told! Is that understood, mister?"

"Perfectly, sir," said the chastized J.G., and you could almost tell how red his face had flushed in the faint light of the binnacle lamp.

Longarm took a deep breath, let half of it out so his voice would stay steady, and said, "I want to be put ashore with my deputy and our prisoner here and now. Like the Indian chief said, I have spoken."

Lieutenant Flynn sounded almost cheerful as he smugly replied, "So have I. I'm in command here, and you'll damned well get off when and where I tell you, see?"

Longarm nodded soberly. "I reckon I do. I was aiming to give you more rope and wait till we all got to Corpus Christi and no doubt some superior Coast Guard officers who weren't in on it. But it was your grand notion to force my hand, so *bueno*, you're under arrest, and I reckon that puts Mister Devereaux here in command, don't it?"

Everyone there but Longarm sucked in his breath the same way. Flynn moved to the far wing of the bridge to fling open some glass and bawl out, "Mutiny! All hands on deck to stand by me and me alone!"

Longarm drew his .44-40 and snapped, "Cut that out before somebody gets hurt! Mister Devereaux, do you mean to take over as I told you to or stand there like a wide-eyed owl?"

Behind him, Deputy Gilbert had his own gun out, suggesting, "I don't like none of these sissy deck-moppers. What say we arrest the whole bunch of 'em, pard?"

Longarm said calmly, "The late Mr. Doyle only named Lieutenant Flynn here as one of his silent partners. I reckon he felt sort of betrayed after his pal laid him low with volley fire after Doyle agreed in Ancient Irish to surrender without a fight!"

"The bastard! You said he'd died without saying anything!" Flynn wailed, more like an old woman than a man.

Longarm shrugged and explained. "I just told you I wanted to let you have more rope. I was anxious to see you hang. For there's nothing lower than a crook who uses a position of trust to cheat. But damn it all, they'll probably let you save your neck by turning in all of the pals you ain't been able to murder yet!"

By this time Chief Tobin was in the hatchway, with a heavy club in one hand, a Navy Colt in the other, and two crewmen backing him up with their Spencers at port arms.

So Flynn snapped, "Arrest these civilians, Chief!"

And Tobin might have tried had not young Devereaux snapped, "Belay that. The lieutenant is under arrest. Escort him to the brig and slap him in irons. After which, helmsman, hard aport and set our course for Corpus Christi. I'll let Commander Wideman worry about this. For as the lieutenant has often reminded me, I'm not paid to do the thinking around here!"

Chapter 15

"But you were bluffing with a rotten hand!" Billy Vail said a week later as he finished reading Longarm's typed-up report in his oak-paneled inner office at the Denver Federal Building.

Longarm just went on lighting his three-for-a-nickel cheroot on his own side of the marshal's cluttered desk. So Vail waved the thin sheets of foolscap like a matador taunting the bull as he insisted, "Don't you stare so innocent at me with your twinkling gray eyes, you goldbrick salesman disguised as a sober lawman! You've admitted right here in your own report that Doyle was dead as a turd in a milk bucket when you reached him after Flynn had laid down a volley of gunfire on his known position. So what would you have done if Flynn had called your bluff aboard that cutter he was commanding that night?"

"I'd have likely gotten off at Brownsville," Longarm replied, shaking out his match. "By then, of course, those steam line officials Flynn had already warned by wire would have covered their own asses pretty good. That's how come I had to tell such fibs to get that damned tub turned around. It didn't take near as long to get on up to Corpus Christi, but by then Lieutenant Flynn had spent enough time in irons, contemplating a court-martial if not a keelhauling, that he was singing like a tweety-bird when his superior Coast Guard officers commenced to question him."

Longarm blew a lazy smoke ring. "They let the Rangers sit in as well, as I put down there in my report. So it didn't take but seventy-two hours and almost that many telegrams up and down the coast before we had most everyone involved in the plot under arrest and squealing on one another like the rats they were. There weren't all that many in on the penny-ante operation, and nobody had ever made enough money to justify even one of the killings. But ain't you ever noticed how it's the cheap crooks who seem stupid enough to kill for next to nothing? Some Rangers who'd been keeping abreast of the beef market assured me the gang was making less'n ten dollars net profit a side on that quarantined beef by the time they'd gone to that much trouble!"

Vail shrugged and blew more pungent cigar smoke back as he pointed out, "They were moving many a side of beef, and with the profits slit less than a score of ways betwixt the crooked shippers and packers, with the help of just one key Coast Guardsman, we're still talking way more money than anyone was making at their more honest jobs. That's if you're certain how many all told were in on it."

Longarm said, "Damn it, I included a carbon of Flynn's signed confession, Boss. As I elaborated more in my official report, it only took a few dedicated bastards. Neither the crews of that steam line nor of that one Coast Guard cutter were in position to question the orders of those few key superiors. It's only up to the skipper and the supercargo where a vessel might or might not put in to load or off-load any damned cargo at any damned time day or night. I put down there how I had to arrest Lieutenant Flynn in front of his first officer to get anyone to question where in thunder Flynn was taking us on a pointless patrol."

Longarm glanced about for an ashtray, saw Vail had ignored his many helpful suggestions as to office furnishings, and calmly fed some tobacco ash to any rug mites by his own big leather chair. Then he continued. "I wasn't bluffing totally. I'd really narrowed down my list of suspects pretty good before Flynn gave his play away. Once I knew what Pryce & Doyle had been

160

up to, I saw right off they'd have never been able to smuggle so brazenly, in bulk, without the help of at least some customs agents."

He took another drag on his smoke, sighed it out, and soberly admitted, "I just wasn't sure who it was at first. You see, Flynn seemed such an asshole I had to consider a junior officer or even a noncom flimflamming him as well as the rest of us."

Vail nodded. "I follow your drift about the crooks being worried when they saw you headed their way. Thanks to all that shit about you in the *Denver Post*, it's an established fact you know your military organization as well as beef, from both sides of the border."

Longarm said modestly, "Anyone who's ever served as an enlisted man knows how often things are really run by the noncoms whilst the officers enjoy their privileges and one another's wives. But I knew fairly soon that Flynn was a petty tyrant who ran things his own way and couldn't abide suggestions. I suspected him seriously after he'd as much as executed Doyle before I could get him to talk. But I didn't know for certain till he had me, Gilbert, and our prisoner on board for that otherwise pointless ride to the Rio Grande."

Longarm flicked more ash and said flatly, "He'd trained his own men not to question his whimsical orders. But I had the advantage of being allowed to consider him an asshole, and mayhaps a better grasp of conflicting jurisdictions in my head. I knew the Coast Guard *had* the mouth of the Rio Grande covered, by others at least as high-ranking as Flynn. So I knew he had no real call to carry me and my own party down the coast that far, unless it was to get us as far as possible from his pals around Corpus Christi Pass."

Marshal Vail scanned something Henry had retyped for Longarm as he nodded his bullet head. "Right, a steamer swinging south from the passage from the open sea would naturally be left to Flynn's station for, what, occasional boarding?"

Longarm nodded and said, "That's about the size of it. Our thin-spread Revenue Service ain't got time to check every

161

known vessel of a familiar line flying the Stars and Stripes. Nobody aboard either ship passing each other in the night would have call to question it when a familiar supercargo told a familiar Coast Guard skipper there was nothing being imported from anywhere in that refrigerated hold. When Flynn agreed there was no need to spill all that artificial cooling out into the balmy gulf air, who was likely to argue? It's all there in one paragraph or another, Boss. Like you said, I'd have never suspected anything myself if they hadn't started acting so suspicious!"

Vail chuckled. "Oh, I don't know about that. Seems I can hardly send you down to the corner for a bucket of beer without you uncovering a gang of bank robbers. But you done us proud this time, old son. Rod Gilbert's on his way to full recovery and Clay Baldwin's on his way to the gallows, whether he gets better or not."

Vail snubbed out his own cigar in the big copper ashtray he kept handy for himself, and set the report aside as he chuckled fondly. "It's still a good thing for you that Coast Guard officer never learned to play cards on an army blanket. He's naturally changed his story a dozen times since you arrested him, and he almost had some higher-ups convinced that you were making up mean things about him. So it's just as well he told that whopper about you before you arrested him instead of after."

Longarm shot his superior a sincerely puzzled frown and asked what they were talking about. So Vail chortled, "Oh, he wired me as well as the Surgeon General's office some cock-and-bull story about you and some government nurse carrying on disgracefully in the officers' quarters down there. Even if a thing like that was true, it surely shows how Flynn had it in for you. He must have known you were closing in on him, right?"

To which Longarm could only reply, "I reckon the poor bastard must have been desperate, making up a whopper like that one!"

Watch for

LONGARM AND THE LAST MAN

184th novel in the bold LONGARM series
from Jove

Coming in April!

SPECIAL PREVIEW!

One was a Yankee gentleman, the other a Rebel hellraiser. They met in a barroom brawl, and the only thing they had in common was a price on their heads—and an aversion to honest work . . .

Texas Horsetrading Co.

Gene Shelton, acclaimed author of *Texas Legends*, brings you a rousing new epic novel of the Wild West.

Here is a special excerpt from this authentic new Western—available from Diamond Books . . .

The last thing Brubs McCallan remembered was a beer bottle headed straight for the bridge of his nose.

Now he came awake in a near panic, a cold, numbing fear that he had gone blind. Beyond the stabbing pain in his head he could make out only jerky, hazy shapes.

Brubs sighed with relief as he realized he was only in jail.

The shapes were hazy and indistinct partly because only a thin, weak light filtered into the cell from the low flame of a guttering oil lamp on a shelf outside the bars. And the shapes were fuzzy partly because his left eye was swollen almost shut.

Brubs leaned back against the thin blankets on the hard wooden cot and groaned. The movement sent the sledgehammer in his head to pounding a fresh set of spikes through his temples.

"Good morning."

Brubs started at the sound of the voice. He tried to focus his good eye on the dim form on the cot across the room. He could tell that the man was tall. His boots stuck out past the end of the cot. He had an arm hooked behind his head for a pillow, his hat pulled down over his eyes. "Mornin' yourself," Brubs mumbled over a swollen lower lip. "Question is, which mornin' is it, anyway?"

"Sunday, I believe. How do you feel?"

"Like I had a boot hung up in the stirrup and got drug over half of Texas." Brubs lifted a hand to his puffy face

167

and heard the scratch of his palm against stubble. "And like somebody swabbed the outhouse with my tongue. Other than that, passin' fair."

"Glad to hear that. I was afraid that beer bottle might have caused some permanent damage."

Brubs swung his feet over the edge of the cot, sat up, and immediately regretted it. The hammer slammed harder against the spikes in his brain. He squinted at the tall man on the bunk across the way. "I remember you," he said after a moment. "How come you whopped me with that beer bottle?"

"I couldn't find an ax handle and you were getting the upper hand on me at the time," the man said.

Brubs wiggled his nose between a thumb and forefinger. "At least you didn't bust my beak again," he said. "That would have plumb made me mad. I done broke it twice the last year and a half. What was we fightin' about?"

The tall man swung his feet over the side of the cot and sat, rubbing a hand across the back of his neck. "You don't remember? After all, you started it."

"Oh. Yeah, I reckon it's comin' back now. But that cowboy was cheatin'. Seen him palm a card on his deal." Brubs snorted in disgust. "Wasn't even good at cheatin'."

"How do you know that?"

"If he'd been any good I wouldn't of caught him. I can't play poker worth a flip. Who pulled him off me?"

"I did."

"What'd you do that for? I had him right where I wanted him. I was hittin' him square in the fist with my face every time he swung. Another minute or two, I'd of had him wore plumb down."

"I didn't want to interfere, but I saw him reach for a knife. That didn't seem fair in a fistfight."

Brubs sighed. "You're dead right about that. That when I belted you?"

"The first time."

Brubs heaved himself unsteadily to his feet. It wasn't easy. Brubs packed a hundred and sixty pounds of mostly muscle on

168

a stubby five-foot-seven frame, and it seemed to him that every one of those muscles was bruised, stretched, or sore. Standing up didn't help his head much, either.

The man on the other bunk raised a hand. "If you don't mind, I'd just as soon not start it again. I don't have a beer bottle with me at the moment."

"Aw, hell," Brubs said, "I wasn't gonna start nothin'. Just wanted to say I'm obliged you didn't let that cowboy stick a knife in my gizzard." He strode stiffly to the side of the bunk and offered a hand. "Brubs McCallan."

The man on the cot stood. He was a head taller than Brubs, lean and wiry, built along the lines of a mountain cat where Brubs tended toward the badger clan. The lanky man took Brubs's hand. His grip was firm and dry. "Dave Willoughby. Nice to make your acquaintance under more civilized conditions."

"Wouldn't call the San Antonio jail civilized," Brubs said with a grin. The smile started his split lower lip to leaking blood again. He released Willoughby's hand. "We tear the place up pretty good?"

"My last recollection is that we had made an impressive start to that end," Willoughby said. "Shortly thereafter, somebody blew the lantern out on me, too."

Both men turned as a door creaked open and bootsteps sounded. The oil lamp outside the cell flared higher as a stocky man twisted the brass key of the wick feeder with a thick hand. The light spilled over a weathered face crowned by an unruly thatch of gray hair. "What's all the yammering about? Gettin' so a man can't sleep around here anymore."

The stocky man stood with the lamp held at shoulder height. A ring of keys clinked as he hobbled to the cell. His left knee was stiff. He had to swing the leg in a half circle when he walked. The lamplight glittered from a badge on his vest and the brass back strap of a big revolver holstered high on his right hip.

"You the sheriff?" Brubs asked.

"Night deputy. Sheriff don't come on duty for another couple hours. Name's Charlie Purvis. If you boys are gonna be the guests of Bexar County for a while, you better learn to keep it quiet when I'm on duty."

"We will certainly keep that in mind, Deputy Purvis," Dave Willoughby said. "We apologize for having disturbed you. We will be more reserved in the future."

Brubs glared through his one open eye at the deputy. "What do you mean, guests of the county?"

"In case you boys ain't heard," the deputy said, "that brawl you started over at the Longhorn just about wrecked the place. I don't figure you two've got enough to pay the fines and damages."

Dave sighed audibly. "How much might that be, Deputy?"

"Twenty-dollar fine apiece for startin' the fight and disturbin' the peace. Thirty-one dollars each for damages. Plus a dime for the beer bottle you busted over your friend's head."

"What?" Brubs's voice was a startled croak. "You gonna charge this man a dime for whoppin' me with a beer bottle?"

The deputy shrugged. "Good glass bottles are hard to find out here. Owner of the Longhorn says they're worth a dime apiece."

Brubs snorted in disgust. "Damnedest thing I ever heard." He glanced up at Willoughby. "Good thing you didn't hit me with the back bar mirror. God knows what that would of cost. You got any money, Dave?"

Willoughby rummaged in a pocket and poked a finger among a handful of coins. "Thirty-one cents."

Brubs sighed in relief. "Good. There for a minute I was afraid we was plumb broke." He fumbled in his own pocket. "I got seventeen cents. Had four dollars when I set in on that poker game."

"Looks like you boys got troubles," Purvis said, shaking his shaggy head. "Can't let you out till the fines and damages are paid."

"How we gonna pay if we're in jail?"

Purvis shrugged. "Should have thought about that before

170

you decided to wreck the Longhorn. Guess you'll just have to work it out on the county farm."

"Farm!" Brubs sniffed in wounded indignation and held out his hands. "These look like farmer's hands?"

The deputy squinted. "Nope. Don't show no sign of work if you don't count the skinned knuckles." Purvis grinned. "They'll toughen up quick on a hoe handle. We got forty acres in corn and cotton, and ten weeds for every crop plant. Pay's four bits a day." He scratched his jaw with a thick finger. "Let's see, now—fifty cents a day, you owe fifty-one dollars. . . . Works out to a hundred and two days. Each."

Dave Willoughby sighed. "Looks like it's going to be a long summer."

Purvis plucked a watch from his vest pocket, flipped the case open, and grunted. "Near onto sunup. You boys wrecked my nap. Might as well put some coffee on." He snapped the watch shut. "I reckon the county can spare a couple cups if you two rowdies want some."

Brubs scrubbed a hand over the back of his neck. "I'll shoot anybody you want for a cup of coffee. Got anything for hangovers? I got a size twelve headache in a size seven head."

The deputy chuckled. "Sympathy's all I got to offer. Know how you feel. I been there, back in my younger days. Busted up a saloon or two myself. You boys sit tight. I'll be back in a few minutes with the coffee."

Brubs trudged back to the cot and sat, elbows propped against his knees. He became aware of a gray light spreading through the cell and glanced at the wall above Dave's bunk. A small, barred rectangle high above the floor brightened with the approaching dawn. "Well, Dave," Brubs said after a moment, "you sure got us in a mess this time."

Willoughby turned to face Brubs, a quizzical expression on his face. "*I* got us in a mess? I was under the impression that you started the fight and I was the innocent bystander."

Brubs shrugged as best he could without moving his throbbing head. "Don't matter. Question now is, how do we break out of here?"

Willoughby raised a hand, palm out. "Wait a minute—you can't be serious! Breaking out of jail is a felony offense. We would be wanted criminals, possibly with a price on our heads. If you're thinking of escape, even if it was possible, count me out."

Brubs prodded his puffy eyebrow with a finger. The swelling seemed to be going down some. "I ain't working for the county, Dave. 'Specially not on some damn farm." He squinted at his free hand. "These hands don't fit no hoe handle. That's how come I left home in the first place."

Willoughby strode to his own bunk and stretched out on his back. "Where's home?"

"Nacogdoches, I reckon. Never had a real home to call it such." He raised his undamaged eyebrow at Willoughby. "You sure talk funny. Since we're tradin' life stories here, where you from?"

"Cincinnati."

"That on the Sabine or the Red River?"

"Neither. It's on the Ohio."

Brubs moaned. "Oh, Christ. I'm sittin' here tryin' my best to die from day-old whiskey, I got my butt whupped in a saloon fight, I owe money I ain't got, I been threatened with choppin' cotton, and now it turns out I'm sharin' a room with a Yankee. If I hadn't had such a damn good time last night, I'd be plumb disgusted."

A faint smile flitted over Willoughby's face. "I suppose it was a rather interesting diversion, at that." He winced and probed the inside of his cheek with his tongue. "I think you chipped one of my teeth. For a little man, you swing a mean punch."

The creak of the door between cell block and outer office brought both men to their feet. Brubs could smell the coffee before the deputy came into view, carrying two tin cups on a flat wooden slab. Purvis crouched stiffly and slid the cups through the grub slot of the cell.

Brubs grabbed a cup, scorched his fingers on the hot tin, sipped at the scalding liquid, and sighed, contented. "Mother's milk for a hungover child," he said. "If I was a preacher I'd bless your soul, Charlie Purvis."

Purvis straightened slowly, the creak of his joints clearly audible. "You boys'll get some half-raw bacon and burnt biscuits when the sheriff gets here. Need anything else meantime?"

"I don't reckon you could see your way clear to leave the key in the lock?" Brubs asked hopefully.

Purvis shook his head. "Couldn't do that." He pointed toward a dark smear on the adobe wall near the door of the office. "Just in case you boys got some ideas perkin' along with the headaches, study on that spot over there. That's what's left of the last man tried to bust out of my jail." He clucked his tongue. "Sure did hate to cut down on him with that smoothbore. Double load of buckshot splattered guts all over the place. Made a downright awful mess. Why, pieces of that fellow were—"

"I think we understand your message, Deputy," Willoughby interrupted with a wince. "If you don't mind, spare us the gory details."

The deputy shrugged. "Well, I'll leave you boys to your chicken pluckin'. Sure don't envy you none. It gets hotter than the devil's kitchen out in those fields in summer."

Brubs moaned aloud at the comment.

"Is there somebody who could help us?" Willoughby asked. "A bondsman, perhaps, or someone who would loan us the money to get out of here?"

Charlie Purvis frowned. "Might be one man. I'm not sure you'd like the deal, though."

"Charlie," Brubs said, pleading, "I'd make a deal with Old Scratch himself to keep my hands off a damn hoe handle."

The deputy shrugged. "Same difference, maybe. But I'll talk to him." Purvis turned and limped away. The door creaked shut behind him.

Brubs stopped pacing the narrow cell and glanced at the small, high window overhead, then at the lean man reclining on the bunk. "How long we been in this place, Dave?"

Willoughby shoved the hat back from over his eyes. "I'd guess a little over half a day."

"Seems a passed longer than that."

"Patience, I gather, is not your strong suit."

Brubs snorted. "Buzzards got patience. All it gets 'em is rotten meat and a yard and a half of ugly apiece." He started pacing again.

"Relax, Brubs," Willoughby said, "you're wasting energy and tiring me out, tromping back and forth like that." He pulled the hat back over his eyes. "Better save your strength for that cotton patch."

Brubs paused to glare at the man on the cot. "You are truly a comfort to a dyin' man, Dave Willoughby. Truly a comfort."

The clomp of boots and the squeak of the door brought Brubs's pacing to a halt. Sheriff Milt Garrison strode to the cell, a big, burly man at his side. The big man seemed to wear more hair than a grizzly, Brubs thought. Gray fur covered most of his face, bristled his forearms, sprouted from heavy knuckles, and even stuck out through the buttonholes on his shirt. For a moment Brubs thought the man didn't have any eyes. Then he realized they were the same color as the hair and were tucked back under brows as thick and wiry as badger bristles.

"These the two Charlie told me about?" The hairy man's voice grated like a shovel blade against gravel.

"That's them." Milt Garrison leaned against the bars of the cell. "Told you they didn't look like much."

"Well, hell," the hairy one said, "if they're tough enough to wreck the Longhorn, maybe they'll do."

"Boys, meet Lawrence T. Pettibone, owner of Bexar and Rio Grande Freight Lines. He's got a deal to offer you." Garrison waved a hand toward the prisoners. "The short one's Brubs McCallan. Other one's Dave Willoughby."

Lawrence T. Pettibone nodded a greeting. "I hear you boys run up a pretty big bill last night. How bad you want to get shut of this place?"

"Mighty bad, Mr. Pettibone," Brubs said.

"All right, here's the deal. I won't say it but once, so you listen careful." Pettibone's smoky eyes seemed to turn harder, like a prize agate marble Brubs remembered from his childhood. "I need two men. You boys got horses and saddles?"

Brubs nodded. "Yes, sir, Mr. Pettibone, we sure do. Over at the livery."

Pettibone snorted. "Probably owe money on them, too."

"Yes, sir. I reckon we owe a dollar apiece board on the mounts."

"You savvy guns?"

Brubs nodded again. "Sure do. I'm a better'n fair hand with a long gun, and I can hit an outhouse with a pistol if it ain't too far off."

"How about you, Willoughby?"

Willoughby's brow wrinkled. "Yes, sir, I can use weapons. If the need arises." His tone sounded cautious.

Pettibone grunted. Brubs couldn't tell if it was a good grunt or a bad grunt. "All right, I guess you two'll do. I was hopin' for better, but a man can't be too picky these days." He pulled a twist of tobacco from a shirt pocket, gnawed off a chew, and settled it in his cheek. "I need two outriders. Guards for a shipment goin' to El Paso day after tomorrow. I'll pay your fines and damages. You ride shotgun for the Bexar and Rio line until you work it off. At a dollar a day."

Brubs sighed in relief. "Dave, that's twice the pay the county offered. And no hoe handles."

"Mr. Pettibone," Willoughby said, "may I inquire as to why you are short of manpower?"

Pettibone twisted his head and spat a wad of tobacco juice. It spanged neatly into a brass cuspidor below the lamp shelf. "Bandits killed 'em last run. Blew more holes in 'em than we could count. Stole my whole damn load."

"Bandits? You mean outlaws?"

Pettibone sighed in disgust. "Now just who the hell else would hold up a freight wagon? A gang of Methodist preachers?"

Willoughby shook his head warily. "I'm not sure about this,

175

Mr. Pettibone. It's one thing to work for a man. It's another matter to possibly have to kill or be killed in the line of work."

Pettibone's gray eyes narrowed. "Suit yourself, son. It don't matter to me. But I need *two* men. Charlie said he figured you two come as a package. Guess I'll have to find me a couple other saddle tramps." He turned and started to walk away.

"Mr. Pettibone, wait a minute," Brubs called. He turned to Dave. "You leave the talkin' to me, Dave," he whispered. "I'm gettin' out of here, and you're goin' with me."

The big man turned back.

"My partner here ain't no lace-drawers type, Mr. Pettibone," Brubs said earnestly. "He's a top hand with a gun and got more guts than a bull buffalo. He just went through some stuff in the war that bothers him time to time. Don't you fret about old Dave." He clapped his cell mate on the shoulder. "You just get us out of here, and we'll make sure your wagon gets through."

Pettibone glared at the two prisoners for several heartbeats, then shrugged. "All right. You're hired." He jabbed a heavy finger at Brubs. "I want you boys to know one thing. I ain't in the charity business. You duck out or turn yellow on me and you'll wish to high hell you were back in this lockup, 'cause I'll skin you out and tan your hides for a pillow to ease my piles, and every time I go to the outhouse I'll take it along to remember you by. Savvy?"

"Yes, sir," Brubs said eagerly, "We savvy. You're the boss."

"Good. Keep that in mind. I'll pick you boys up tomorrow afternoon." He turned to walk away.

"Mr. Pettibone?"

"Now what, McCallan?"

Brubs swallowed. "Reckon you could get us out today? No disrespect to Bexar County or this fine sheriff here, but this ain't the most comfortable jail I ever been in. I sure would like to get my stuff in shape and take the kinks out of my sorrel before we move out."

Pettibone glowered at Brubs for a moment. "Damned if you

boys don't try a man's patience something fierce. All right, I'll get you out now. You got any place to stay?"

"No, sir, Mr. Pettibone."

Pettibone's massive chest rose and fell. Brubs thought he saw the hair in the big man's ears bristle. "You can bunk in at my place. Cost you a dollar a day apiece. I'll add it onto what it's going to cost me to spring the pair of you. Damn, but the cost of help's gettin' high these days." Pettibone turned to the sheriff. "Cut 'em loose, Milt."

Brubs heaved a deep sigh of relief as the key turned in the cell lock and the barred door swung open. He knew it was the same air outside the cell as in, but it still smelled better. He and Willoughby fell into step behind the sheriff and Pettibone.

Brubs and Willoughby waited patiently as Lawrence T. Pettibone frowned at the column of figures on Sheriff Milt Garrison's ledger. "What the hell's this ten cents for a beer bottle?"

"Dave busted one over my head, Mr. Pettibone," Brubs said.

Pettibone snorted in disgust. "Damnedest thing I ever heard," he growled. "Chargin' a man for bustin' a beer bottle in a saloon brawl."

"Sort of the way I figured it, Mr. Pettibone," Brubs said earnestly. "Pricin' a man's fun plumb out of sight these days."

"I ain't payin' for no damn bottle," Pettibone said. "No way I can figure how to get ten cents worth of work out of two guys on a dollar a day."

Brubs dug in a pocket and produced a coin. "Give me a nickel, Dave. We'll split the cost of the bottle."

Pettibone finally grunted and pulled a wad of bills from a pocket. Brubs's eyes went wide at the sight of the roll. It was more money than he'd seen in one place since the big horse race up in Denton. Pettibone licked a thumb and counted out the bills, sighing as he caressed each one. Pettibone acted like he was burying a sainted mother every time he put a dollar on the desk, Brubs thought.

Garrison gathered up the bills, dropped the money in a tin box, and scribbled a receipt. He handed the paper to Pettibone, then retrieved the prisoners' weapons from a locked closet. "Guess you bought yourself some shotgun riders, Lawrence," he said.

Pettibone cast a cold glance at Brubs and Willoughby. "Don't know if I bought a good horse or a wind-broke plug," he groused. "I sure as hell hope they ride and shoot better than they smell. You boys are a touch ripe. There's a big water tank out by my wagon barn. Wouldn't hurt either of you to muzzle up to some soap. Now, strap them gun belts on and let's go bail your horses out of the lockup."

Willoughby paused for a moment, rotated the cylinder of his Colt, and raised an eyebrow. "Should we go ahead and load the chambers now, Mr. Pettibone?" he asked.

Pettibone groaned aloud. "Fools. I just bought two idiots with my hard-earned money. Dammit, son, what good's an unloaded pistol?" He watched in disgust as Willoughby thumbed cartridges into the Colt and reached for his Winchester rifle. "I guess you boys got plenty of ammunition?"

"I got ten rifle cartridges," Brubs said, shoving loads into his scarred Henry .44 rimfire long gun. "Maybe a dozen for the pistol."

"I have half a box of .44-40's," Willoughby said. "Same caliber fits both my handgun and rifle."

Pettibone snorted in disgust. "Damn. Now I've got to lay out some more hard cash on you two. My men don't ride with less than a hundred rounds each. Come on—we'll stop off at the general store down the street."

The two men fell into step behind Pettibone. A few minutes later the hairy one emerged from the store, four boxes of ammunition in a big hand. "I'll add the cost of the shells to your bill, boys. Fifty cents a box."

"Fifty cents? Mr. Pettibone, that's a dime more than I paid anywhere," Brubs said, incredulous.

"Call it a nuisance fee," Pettibone growled, "because you boys are nuisances if I ever seen 'em. Course, if you'd rather work it out with the county—"

"No, sir," Brubs said quickly. "I reckon that's fair enough.

We won't nuisance you no more."

"I doubt that." Pettibone spat a wad of used-up tobacco into the street. "Let's get home before you two drifters cost me my last dollar."

"Mr. Pettibone?"

"What now, McCallan?"

"Any chance we could get a bottle of whiskey added to our bill?"

"No, by God!" Pettibone bellowed. "Don't push your luck, boy, or you'll be behind a hoe handle all summer!"

"Yes, sir," Brubs said. "But it was worth a try."

A half hour later, Brubs and Willoughby rode side by side behind Lawrence T. Pettibone's buggy. Brubs forked a big, rangy sorrel, and Dave rode a leggy black that looked to have some Tennessee racing stock in his bloodline.

"Brubs," Willoughby said quietly, "I have the distinct impression that our new employer is somewhat thrifty with his funds."

Brubs flashed a quick grin. "I reckon he can squeeze a peso until the Mexican eagle looks like a plucked crow."

Lawrence T. Pettibone's combination home and wagon yard and adjoining stock pastures spread over most of a section on the northern outskirts of San Antonio.

Brubs had to admit he was impressed. The corrals were sturdy, fenced by peeled logs the size of a man's thigh, and watered by a big windmill that creaked as it whirred in the southwest breeze. The barn was as solidly built as the corrals, expansive and well ventilated. The main house was big, and built of real cut lumber, not adobe or split logs.

Brubs was even more impressed with what came from inside the big house.

Pettibone pushed the door open, growled at Brubs and Willoughby to wait on the porch, and went inside. He was back a minute later with a stiff-bristled brush and a bar of lye soap in hand, and one of the prettiest girls Brubs had seen west of Savannah trailing behind.

179

The girl was blond. Palomino hair tumbled past her shoulders, dancing gold in the warm afternoon sunshine. The pale rose housedress she wore wrapped itself around a figure that made Brubs want to paw the ground and snort. Her eyes were big, blue, and had a smoldering look about them above a perky, upturned nose. She looked to be about twenty. This, Brubs knew instinctively, was one hot-blooded woman. He swept the battered and stained hat from his head.

"Boys, this here is Callie, my daughter," Pettibone said. "Callie, these two bums'll be riding shotgun for us a spell. Don't shoot 'em for prowlers until I get my money back out of 'em. The little feller's name is Brubs McCallan. The tall one's Dave Willoughby."

Brubs bowed deep at the waist, then grinned at the blonde. He wished for a moment he had just had a bath and shave; some women were mighty picky about that, as if it made some sort of difference. "Mighty pleased to make your acquaintance, Miss Pettibone," Brubs said. "A pretty girl does brighten a poor saddle tramp's day."

"Lay a hand on Callie and I'll kill you," Pettibone said. It wasn't exactly a threat, Brubs noted. More like a statement of fact.

Brubs tore his gaze from the girl and glanced at his cell mate. Willoughby had removed his hat, but merely nodded a greeting. He did not speak.

A second woman, a Mexican somewhere in her late twenties, appeared at the door. She was a bit thick of hip and waist, her upper lip dusted by scattered but distinct black hairs. Overall though, not bad looking, Brubs decided. Away from the blonde she might even be pretty.

"That's Juanita. She's the cook and maid." Pettibone held out the brush and lye soap. "Long as I'm makin' introductions, this is stuff to clean up with. Put your horses in the barn and yourselves in that water tank out back, or don't come in for supper."

Brubs hesitated, reluctant to leave the warm glow that seemed to spread in all directions from Callie, until he realized that

Lawrence T. Pettibone was glaring a hole through him. Brubs quickly replaced his hat, turned away, and mounted with a flourish, swinging into the saddle without touching a stirrup. He wasn't above showing off a bit when a pretty girl was watching. He kneed his sorrel gelding around and set off after Willoughby, who was already leading his leggy black toward the barn thirty yards away.

"Man, ain't she something?" Brubs said as he reined in alongside Willoughby. "I ain't seen a filly like that my whole life through. Prime stuff, that Callie."

Willoughby cast a worried glance at Brubs. "You heard what Pettibone said, Brubs. You'd better leave the girl alone."

Brubs chuckled aloud. "Just adds a little spice to the puddin', my Yankee friend. You see the way Callie was lookin' at me? Her eyes got all smoky-like."

"I saw the way Pettibone was looking at you." Willoughby swung the corral gate open.

"Ah, that inflated tadpole ain't much to worry about," Brubs said.

"I worry about a lot of things, Brubs. One of which is that if you try messing around with that girl, somebody is likely to get hurt. Like you and me."

Brubs reached down and cuffed Dave on the shoulder. "Don't you fret, Dave. You just watch ol' Brubs work that herd, you'll learn somethin' about handlin' women."

"And that," Willoughby said solemnly, "is exactly what's bothering me. I'm beginning to wonder if perhaps Brubs McCallan wasn't put on this earth just to get one Dave Willoughby killed."

If you enjoyed this book, subscribe now and get...

TWO FREE

A $7.00 VALUE—

LONGARM

Explore the exciting Old West with
one of the men who made it wild!